SOPHIE'S CAT

about the author

Billi Rosen was born in Greece, where she spent her early childhood. She was educated in Sweden and moved to the United Kingdom in her late teens. She subsequently travelled extensively in Europe, living in Italy, Switzerland and on the Greek island of Corfu. She has since returned to England and now lives in London. She has worked in education, in television, and as a freelance photographer and journalist. Her first book for children, *Andi's War*, won the Faber/Guardian/Jackanory Children's Writers Competition in 1987, and since its first publication in the UK it has been translated into fourteen languages. *The Other Side of the Mountain* is its sequel.

by the same author

ANDI'S WAR
THE OTHER SIDE OF THE MOUNTAIN

SOPHIE'S CAT

Billi Rosen

illustrated by
Carol Binch

First published in 1991
by Faber and Faber Limited
3 Queen Square London WC1N 3AU

Printed in England by Clays Ltd, St Ives plc

A CIP record for this book is available from the British Library

ISBN 0 571 16941 4

2 4 6 8 10 9 7 5 3 1

Preface

Upper Catsfield clings to the hillside like a barnacle to the side of a ship or fleas to a dog. Surrounded by golden fields, meadows purple with bluebells, clover, frail forget-me-nots, woods starred with anemones, it is a hamlet, a collection of cottages and farms with a short high street, bordered by an avenue of leafy chestnut trees. There is a church, a green with a pond at one end and a cricket pavilion at the other and, a little apart from it all, an old stone wall. Thought to be Roman, the wall is home to a rich variety of creepy-crawlies, a fact well known to the local children, who for generations have descended on it, armed with jam-jars and matchboxes. It is also a favourite rendezvous for the district's cats, whose raucous love calls, especially between January and March, have everyone gnashing their teeth and stopping their ears.

Some say that the cats gave the place its name: back in the Middle Ages, when the Black Death was sweeping the country, cutting down whole populations like stalks of corn at harvest time, hundreds of cats are said to have surrounded the hamlet, cutting it off from the rest of the world and the invading rats, enabling people to escape the Grim Reaper. The inhabitants, grateful to their feline saviours, named their hamlet after them and declared them free from persecution for all time – this in an age when cats were believed to be familiars of the Devil, the companions of witches (riding on brooms, casting spells, bringing bad luck), and, more often than not, were burned at the stake with their owners. Welcomed at firesides once again, the cats grew so numerous that no rat or mouse ever dared to show its face in Catsfield.

Those who don't believe this story say that it was put about by the ancestors of the present Misses Boone, all of them great cat lovers, to ensure the safety of their pets. Whether this is true or not, no cat has ever been wilfully destroyed in Upper Catsfield and anyone found to have brought about the demise of one, even accidentally, is a jerk!

But back to Catsfield. The village, then as now, was situated half of it on the hill, half of it at the hill's foot, hugging the main road to I'chester, and connected only by a steep, rough, stony, badly pitted, unmade lane. That hasn't changed, though much else has. With the passage of time the two halves grew apart. In the end, as was bound to happen, they dropped all pretence of being one village and went their separate ways. To distinguish one from the other they added 'Upper' and 'Lower' to their common name. By now they have nothing, or next to nothing, to say to each other and, were it not for the fact that Upper Catsfield is too small to have its own school, they might have gone so far as to ignore each other completely.

As Upper Catsfield is such a solitary spot, and glad of it, the pace of life there is slow and positively sedate. This suits the very young and the very old, and plenty of in-betweens too, but there is one group, made up of eight boisterous youngsters in their best if not most sensible years, who, though not troublemakers in the real sense of the word, always welcome an opportunity to ripple the waters of the pond.

Sprat and Titch (Charlie Biggs and his sister Alison, ten and eight respectively) are both small, pale, mousy, agile as monkeys and tough as old boots. Then there's Indy (Idira Macawbee, nine and a half), who has skin a delicious chocolate colour, a head of tight black curls and large luminous brown eyes – a thoughtful girl, kind and softly spoken.

The Squire (ten and three-quarters), real name Alexander Fox-Smythe, has flaming red hair and lives at the Manor. A good sort who'd never think of giving himself airs, he does come to school in the family Rolls from time to time (mostly because he's missed the bus). His parents want him to go to boarding school but he's told them he doesn't want to and if they send him he'll only run away.

Busker (Nicky Paige, nine) got his nickname because he's always strumming on an imaginary guitar. His dream is to go to London and play in the underground. As for Archie Williams (nine and two months), he is champion TV-zealot, sold on Space Soap and anything extra-terrestrial.

Kid Brown (almost eleven), thin face, tangled brown hair and defiant, sky-blue eyes, is quiet, self-contained and kind of down to earth, though he is inclined to sudden sharp flashes of temper. He is often at odds with Archie Williams, because if Archie steps out of line, Kid generally does something about it. His dad is the local cop.

Sophie Miller (ten) is slight and freckled, with warm, lively, brown eyes and corn-yellow hair. Impish, bright and impulsive, she tends to act on the spur of the moment. Like Kid and Archie, she is called by her real name, though the others sometimes refer to her as 'Brains'.

1

Kid Brown waits by the gate for Sophie Miller to turn up so they can start for school. With him is his dog, Smith, a golden retriever whose job it is to go with the children in the morning and fetch them home again in the afternoon – this is because Kid and Sophie insist on walking rather than going in the school bus with the other children.

They walk partly because Kid says it's the only time he gets to play with Smith – both have plenty of chores waiting for them at home – and partly because it's a good time to talk about all kinds of things, like friends, school and, of course, parents. Kid's line is that his don't understand him. Sophie says hers are all right and that though they can be ever so irritating at times, on the whole it's no real hardship putting up with them.

Kid thinks her very lucky. His mother and father are all negatives when it comes to him. They didn't even give him a proper name. Kid! Even so, it's rarely used at home. Instead he is: lazy-bones, slowcoach, butterfingers, blister, baggage, misery, Mister. It's not fair! He knows he could be different, given half a chance – not long-faced and 'obstinate-mulish', as his father calls it, but happy, helpful, fun and clever too. Not like Sophie, who is good at school, but in his own way: he can carve anything out of wood, draw, paint, toss pancakes, make an omelette, bring up baby birds abandoned by their parents or fallen out of the nest, make splints for the tiniest bones and he has the greenest fingers ever. Even seasoned gardeners put pride to one side and seek his help when something they've planted just won't come up. Kid will put his ear to the ground, listen, place his hands where the seeds have been sown, hum softly (any tune will do), gently turn the earth with his fingers and, hey presto, only days later tiny green shoots appear as if by magic, pleased as Punch at their first worm's eye view of the sky. And people will stare at the formerly barren patch of ground, scratch their heads and mumble: 'That Kid! Now there's a boy who knows a good trick or two when it comes to growing things.'

But this kind of praise only ever comes from others, never from his parents. They really don't seem to know what a treasure they have right under their noses. And because Kid feels his parents don't know him, he sometimes doesn't know himself. It's all very confusing. Sophie, a dab hand with words, once put it like this:

Kid Blister
Kid Baggage
Kid Slowcoach
Kid Trouble

Kid Round
Kid Square
Kid Happy
Kid Sad

Who is Kid?

Kid pulls a face. He is still working it out!

He glances down at his watch. That Sophie. For weeks now, ever since Snowflake, the farm cat, dropped her new litter, waiting for Sophie has been like waiting for Christmas.

Kid jumps over the gate, then opens it to let Smith through. 'Come on, we've got to get going,' he tells him. 'Miss Bradley said if we roll in late once more this term she'll have to send a note home about it. Don't know about Soph, but my dad, he'll have me cleaning out the chicken run with a toothbrush or something.'

The Browns run a small free-range egg and poultry farm. At least, Mrs Brown does. Mr Brown is the local constable, though he does double as egg-man when off duty.

As the gate clicks to behind him Kid automatically looks in the direction Sophie is due to appear from . . . and there she is, a small figure in a red-and-white candy-striped dress, looking like a stick of Brighton rock on the run. Puffing and panting, she comes to an abrupt stop beside Kid and leans forward, hands on knees, to catch her breath.

'At last,' he scolds her. 'You'll get us into real trouble, you will.'

'Sorry, but I just had to see the kittens before I went,' Sophie wheezes.

'They'll still be there when you get back.'

'I know, but it's ages till then. If you like, I'll tell Miss Bradley it's my fault we've been coming late.'

'Think I'd hide behind a girl, do you?' he snaps at her.

'No.'

'Then why come with something daft like that. I don't need anyone to stand up for me.'

'Keep your shirt on, Kid Brown! Just give me a mo to build up some steam and we'll be off.'

'Just as well we're going down the lane or you'd not make it to school at all, the way you're puffing,' Kid says tersely.

Sophie doesn't take any notice of her friend's acid tone. It's only old Kid letting off steam.

2

The day which began bright and sunny slowly turns a dull, heavy grey. The minute school is over the first drops of rain begin to fall. By the time the bus draws up outside the school gates, it is raining cats and dogs.

Kid thrusts his chin towards it. 'Want to take it?' he asks Sophie.

She shrugs her shoulders. 'Not bothered.'

'Me neither.'

Their friends, already in the bus, shake their heads at the mad duo outside. Walk, when one can ride? Never catch them doing anything so daft! Except for going to Saturday morning cinema, walking is definitely OUT. And even then they are sometimes lucky enough to get a lift on a tractor or on the back of a milk or potato cart.

The bus moves up the narrow lane, sides scraping against hawthorn and bramble. Rumbling and rattling, it begins its climb to the top. A judder, a shudder, a sharp swing to the left, then to the right, and it's gone. Sophie and Kid stand and watch until it has disappeared from view. Now it's gone they almost wish they'd taken it. Sophie gives the dark sky a sour look. 'Didn't look like rain this morning,' she mutters.

'Would have brought my mac if I'd thought it'd turn out like this,' Kid replies crossly.

Sophie says she watched the weather on TV before going to bed last night and there wasn't anything about rain – not a whisper, not the tiniest clue, like 'sunny intervals' or 'clouds moving in from the west' or 'deepening depressions'.

Kid pushes back some strands of wet hair that are sticking to his forehead. 'Those guys never, ever get it right,' he spits.

They embark on the long uphill climb in silence. In no time at all they, Smith included, look like drowned rats. To take their minds off the weather, they start throwing sticks for Smith. It works, at least as far as Smith's concerned. They throw, he bounds after them, brings them back. They throw again, he fetches again, and so it goes. The game distracts them for a while, but soon it begins to pall. Things really don't look too bright when all of a sudden Sophie says: 'Kid, do you remember what we used to do on wet days when we were small?'

Kid swings his arm back, brings it forward in an arch over his head and lets go of the stick. 'Can't say I do.'

'We had this game we called "Jumping puddles". Remember?'

To begin with Kid looks blank, then his face lights up in a wide grin. 'Yeah, now you mention it . . .'

'Well?'

'I'm game if you are.'

'You bet.'

'Sophie Miller,' Kid goes on, 'you are brilliant, even if you are a girl. I forgive you for being late this morning . . . and yesterday . . . and last week and all the times before that.'

'Thanks.'

'Where do we start?'

'Over there.'

'That one?'

'Yup.'

'You do mean the one that looks like the English Channel?'

'Yup.'

'We might not make it.'

'Only one way to find out.'

'Right. Well, here goes! On your marks, get set . . . GO!'

The puddle turns out to be considerably wider than it had seemed at first. Only Smith makes it across without getting his feet wet.

Kid stares down at his waterlogged shoes. 'Wow. What a start!'

Sophie kicks hers off, empties the water out and slips them back on. 'Ready for the next one?' she asks Kid.

'I am if you are.'

'Which one now?'

'Let's take them as they come . . . this one . . . that one . . . all of them!'

'OK!'

A moment's hesitation, then . . . Jumping puddles might get them into even deeper water, so to speak,

but it does take the sting out of the gritty climb.

'Beats the bus any time,' Sophie shouts.

'Archie doesn't know what he's missing,' Kid returns at the top of his voice, ankle-deep in yet another puddle of dirty brown water.

'Maybe we should get him to try it. Show him what legs are for.'

'Waste of effort. Archie's got it bad.'

'What?'

'Square-eyes . . . box-on-the-brain . . . technicolour blindness. You name it, he's got it!'

'Yeah! But it's not just Archie. The other kids are just as bad. If it wasn't for Saturday morning cinema, none of them would use their legs from one week to the next.'

'More fool them!' Kid stops so abruptly that Sophie, directly behind, crashes into him.

'What is it?'

Kid points. 'Look at that! You ever seen a puddle like it?'

Sophie stares at the huge area of water ahead. Some puddle! A pool of oceanic proportions!

'Holy St Christopher!' she squawks.

'A body can't be expected to pass up such a challenge.' Kid whistles.

'No way!'

'There'll be plenty of stick at home if we don't clear it.'

'Worth it, though.'

'In for a penny, in for a pound, right?'

'Right,' Sophie hollers, and then goes on:

'In for a penny,
In for a pound,
Throw him in and
Watch him drown!'

'Who?' Kit wants to know.

'No one,' she says. Then, thoughtfully, 'but if it did have to be someone, then the one I'd chuck in would be that big, ugly man who's moved into Yew Tree Farm. Stone, or whatever his name is.'

'Me too. Anyway' – Kid pulls a face – 'let's not talk about him. Let's jump. One, two, three!'

The take-off is perfect, but not so the landing. Sophie and Kid, up to their waists in mud and water (Smith between them), take stock of the situation. They can't remember being so utterly and thoroughly SOAKED.

'I can just picture my mum's face when Smith and I come through the door,' Kid muses. 'I'll get what for, that's certain.'

'I might just get off. With luck my mum will be in her shed, bent deep over her workbench, when I get in. Still, better get out of this before we begin to grow fins and tails.'

'And gills too,' Kid laughs.

Clinging to one another for support, they eventually manage to get out of the mud. They waddle the last bit up to the top of the lane, water pouring off them in torrents. A few more minutes and they are in front of Kid's gate. 'Well, that's me home,' he says.

Sophie sighs. 'Wish I was. Well, see you.'

Kid, one leg already over the gate, lets himself down on the other side.

'Hey, Soph!'

'What?'

'Think your dad will let you keep a kitten this time?'

Sophie twists her mouth and shakes her head. 'Not a chance,' she says emphatically. 'Short of a miracle, nothing will change his mind about having a cat in the house!'

'Miracles don't exactly grow on trees. At least not hereabouts,' says Kid, who often wishes for one himself.

Sophie is making ready to go when something small and white dashes across the lane and into the adjoining barley field, closely pursued by a huge dog and a big hulk of a man with a gun. In spite of the rain, he is only partly dressed, as if he's come out in a real hurry. He is bareheaded, his shirt is hanging out of his trousers, his braces, meant to hold both in order, flapping at his sides. His lumpish face is wild with rage: the eyes, pinned on the hapless little animal fleeing through the barley, burn with fury and the mouth is compressed into a thin white line.

'Farmer Stone,' Sophie whispers, awed by the sight of the man.

Kid shoots a thin jet of saliva through the gap in his front teeth. 'Now there's a toad,' he says, putting plenty of sting into it, 'a real blot on the landscape. That's what Dad says of him , anyway.'

'That man's not happy unless he can point his gun at something. Just look at him. Doesn't even take the time to dress properly. Well, I hope he gets pneumonia and dies,' Sophie ends bitterly. 'I for one won't shed any tears for him.'

Just then a shot rings out, quickly followed by another. The two children wince. 'Poor little thing,' Sophie says sadly, thinking of the small white blur.

'Ogre!' Kid snarls. 'One day someone will turn a gun on him and then we'll see how he likes it. I wonder why he moved here?'

'Don't know, but I wish he hadn't.'

'He has not spoken to anyone from the village or asked anyone to Yew Tree Farm since he took it over.'

'And those boards he's put up. It's "Keep Out", "No Trespassers", "Beware of the Dog" . . .'

'Wonder why he's so eager to keep people out? You'd think, coming to a new place, he'd be anxious to make friends with everyone.'

'Mum swears she's not come across him in the shops either. I mean, he must buy food and go to the post office and things.'

'He sure seems keen to keep his head down.'

'You think the law is after him?'

'Don't be daft. If that was true, he'd not advertise himself by putting up those boards, would he? Besides, I would have heard of it from my dad.'

'Well, one day he'll do something really bad and then your dad *will* get him.'

'Like what?'

'Kill a cat, for instance.'

'You can't pull someone in for just killing a cat. Even here.'

'Someone's pet, then.'
'He's already done that.'
Sophie is aghast. 'Whose?'
'Farmer Jones's red setter, Jack. The old man is really cut up about it.'
'Who says he killed him?'
'My dad. He heard it in the pub.'
'Then why doesn't he arrest him?'
'Because they haven't found Jack's body. No body, no proof. No proof, no arrest.'
'Someone should take his gun and break it over his head,' Sophie puffs indignantly. 'If he has killed Jack, then someone knows, only they are afraid to say so. People are scared of him because of his gun. He'd be nothing without it. Just a big, ugly bully. That's what I think anyway.'
'Me too.'
'And then there's 'The Beast'. That dog of his and the Hound of the Baskervilles are one and the same if you ask me.'
'Yeah. And I happen to know he starves it and beats it and, apart from when he takes it with him hunting, he keeps it on a chain this long.'
Kid measures out a very short length of imaginary chain and holds it up for Sophie to 'see'.
'How do you know that?'
'I got it from Mum and she got it from Rita, the barmaid at The White Cat.'
'Oh, but you can't trust anything *she* says.' Sophie is dismissive. 'You know what a muckraker she can be.'
'I know, but when it comes to the Ogre, I'm ready to believe all I hear.'

'Same here, but only as long as it doesn't come from her. Personally, I don't set great store by someone who walks about with a murdered animal on their back.'

'Perhaps she had that coat before everyone got all hot and bothered about fur coats.'

'Perhaps she did, but that's not the point, is it?' Sophie corrects him.

'Suppose not,' Kid concedes.

By now they are so cold that their teeth are knocking together. Kid begins to walk backwards up the drive. 'Time to face the music, I guess.'

'Yup. Anyway, come over if you can. I think Dad's baking again this weekend.'

Kid licks his lips. 'Mmmm . . . home-made bread.'

'With lashings of cherry jam,' Sophie tempts him.

'Cut it out. You're making me drool. I'll try, but you know how it is with us at weekends. All work and no play. My folks think I get to play enough during the week. Dad's got a right bee in his bonnet about it. Says that's all kids ever do at school now and how much tougher it was in his day.'

'Grown-ups always think things were harder for them than they are for us,' Sophie says. 'Anyway, try and come.'

'You bet.'

'Cheers.'

3

Home at last, Sophie kicks off her mud-caked shoes and starts towards her room on tiptoe, leaving a trail of wet footprints behind her. She's just passing the kitchen when her father's voice rings out: 'That you, Sophie?'

She stops and takes a deep breath. What must be must be. She goes to the door and says meekly, 'I didn't know you were in.'

Her father, elbow-deep in dough, stares at her, eyes bulging, mouth wide open. Sophie rests her brown eyes on him and waits, a small pool of water slowly forming at her feet. Mr Miller lifts his arms out of the dough and brings his hands together, as if pleading for strength from some superior power.

'Your mum will tear a right strip off you for this,' he rumbles. 'Come to that, I've got a good mind to do it myself.'

'Yes, Dad,' Sophie replies in the same meek tones as before, her face a mask (a very muddy one) of angelic repentance. She discovered long ago that a humble, 'Yes, sir; no, sir' is by far the best way to defuse a potentially explosive situation.

'I thought we'd agreed it wouldn't happen again,'

Mr Miller says, clearly referring to the last time she came home in such a state.

'Yes, Dad. Sorry, Dad. But, Dad, that was years and years ago.' She wipes her face with the back of her hand, spreading the mud more evenly over her cheeks and chin. Her father shakes his head.

'Best get out of those clothes before you catch your death,' he says, looking sorrowfully at her mud-splattered dress. Then, helplessly: 'How the devil do you manage to get into such a state?'

'Easy, Dad.'

'You making fun of me, girl?'

'No, Dad. Honest!'

He glowers at her, not certain how to respond. Eventually, he says, 'You should have taken a mac with you this morning.'

'There was no need to. The morning was all sunny.' Anxious to inform him she wasn't alone in not anticipating the change in weather, she adds: 'Kid didn't have one either. We both got soaked through.'

'Evidently!'

And now the worst is over, Sophie thinks she might as well come clean. 'We jumped every puddle in the lane, Dad. It was great!'

'Just don't expect any sympathy if you go down with a cold.'

'No, Dad. Only if I die.'

Mr Miller stares hard into the dough. Anyone who knows him well, like Sophie here, would say he's having a job keeping a straight face. Sophie skips up to him and gives him a quick peck on the cheek.

'What brought that on?'

'Nothing, I just felt like it.'

'Well, thank you, dear.'

'I'm glad you're baking.'

Mr Miller goes back to kneading the dough. 'Hurry up and get out of those wet things now.'

'Yes, Dad. Dad?'

'When you've changed.'

'I love you, Dad.'

'I love you too, sweetheart.'

'Dad?'

'What is it now?'

'It's about Stone . . .'

'When you've changed. And, Sophie . . .'

She looks at him expectantly. 'Yes, Dad?'

'It's *Farmer* Stone.'

'Yes, Dad. Dad?'

He lets out a groan. 'What now?'

'May I have one of . . .'

'I said change!'

She goes, happy to have got away so lightly. As for Stone – Farmer Stone indeed! She can't understand her father. Why should she be polite about someone who so far hasn't shown the slightest respect for anyone?

4

A while later Sophie, now in dry clothes and with her hair brushed, jogs back to the kitchen, just as her father is putting the first batch of bread into the oven.

'How long before it's ready? I'm starving!'

'Be a while, I'm afraid.'

'Shall I get the table ready for tea?'

'If you like.'

Sophie wipes down the top of the round wooden table (made by her mother, like most of their furniture) and then goes on to put out cups and saucers, bread plates, knives, teaspoons, milk, butter and, lastly, right at the centre of the table, the dappled blue stoneware jar containing the cherry jam.

'This all right?' she asks her father.

He looks it over to see if she's forgotten anything. She hasn't.

'That's fine,' he tells her. 'Your mum will be pleased to come in and find it all done.'

'Where is she?'

'In her shed, I think.'

'What is she making now?'

'A bookcase, or maybe it's a sideboard. I'm not sure which.'

'She's clever at making things, isn't she, Dad?'

'She is. Me, I'm all thumbs when it comes to hammers and screwdrivers.'

'But you cook and make bread and that's just as good,' Sophie consoles him.

'I think people should stick to what they're best at,' her father answers. 'Your mother is a wizard at woodwork, and I'm a wizard at cooking and making bread. She doesn't tell me how to knead the dough and I don't tell her how to work the wood.'

Sophie giggles. 'Remember that time you changed over? The stool you made collapsed the first time you sat on it, and Mum's loaves were like bricks.'

'Like I said. You should stick to what you're good at.'

'Dad, may I have a slice of the bread as soon as it's out of the oven?'

'It'll give you indigestion.'

'I don't care. It's worth it.'

'Like getting yourself soaked jumping puddles, eh?' He grins.

Just then her mother walks in. 'Hello, darlings,' she beams. 'Tea ready yet?' She gives them both a kiss, then goes over to the sink to rinse her hands. She and Sophie sit down while Mr Miller pulls on a pair of oven gloves.

'Here it comes, folks!'

'Mum, Mum! May I have the crust. May I, please?'

'You want both or just one?' her mother asks. Sophie feels the colour rush to her cheeks. Three people, two crusts. Three into two won't go.

'I know,' she says. 'Let's share them.'

'Thank you, darling. It's very nice of you to share with us. We do so love crust.'

Sophie, feeling really generous now, offers to give them her share too. Her mum says it's all right, she only wants a small piece. Sophie throws her arms around her, and draws a deep breath. Aaah . . . All of Mrs Miller – her clothes, her skin, her hair have about them a permanent smell of pine forests.

Later, when tea's over, Sophie tells them what she and Kid saw earlier on in the lane.

'Kid is sure it was a rabbit but I think it was something else.'

'Probably was a rabbit. Plenty about now,' her father says.

'That doesn't mean he has to shoot them.'

'Kinder in the long run than some other ways.'

'Farmer Stone doesn't do it to be kind. He enjoys killing them.'

'Fact is, people are grateful to Farmer Stone for keeping the rabbits down, even if they don't like him personally.' He ruffles her still-damp hair. 'Perhaps the rabbit you saw got away,' he says kindly.

Her mother gives a snort. 'Stone's not one to miss his target, darling.'

'He's horrible' Sophie says. 'Always with a gun, always on the lookout for something to kill.'

'Steady on,' her father says.

'Well, it's true. He shot old Jones's Jack, didn't he?'

'It's true Jack's gone, but that's not to say Farmer Stone shot him,' her father points out.

'He shouldn't be allowed to carry a gun about.'

'Farmer Stone has a licence for that gun. As long as he doesn't take it into his head to start threatening people with it, he can use it all he likes.'

'Still,' Mrs Miller says thoughtfully, 'I agree with Sophie. There is a bad feel about that man.'

'All the kids think he's an ogre,' Sophie volunteers.

'Bogeyman too, eh?'

'We think he might be hiding from the police.'

'I don't believe it's anything as dramatic as that.' Her father laughs, then adds, 'You kids are letting your imaginations run wild with Farmer Stone.'

'Bet you would too if you were us.'

While he is thinking of an answer to this she comes out with something else:

> 'Ugly old Stone,
> Face like a baboon,
> Put him in a cage
> And take him to the zoo!'

Her parents stare at her, aghast. 'Sophie!'

'Well . . .'

'You should be polite about people . . . even if you don't happen to like them,' her father says sternly.

'Why?'

'Well . . . er . . . because.'

'Did Gran and Grandad tell you to be polite about people you didn't like when you were young?'

'Well now. Let me see . . .'

Mrs Miller nods. 'I'm certain my parents did.'

'And did you?'

Sophie waits, her brown eyes scanning their faces

for a glimpse of the girl and the boy who grew up to become her mother and father.

'I think so,' her mother says tentatively.

'Me too,' her father slips in. 'From what I remember, I was a well-behaved little boy.'

Sophie lets it go. She's sure they've got everything wrong. She doesn't believe either of them was as good as they are trying to make out. She decides the time has come to change the subject.

'Dad, please may I have one of Snowflake's kittens?'

'What was that?' her father says, still miles away, thinking about when he was a boy.

'I want a kitten. May I have one of Snowflake's kittens?'

'Now, Sophie. You know how I feel about animals in the house.'

Mr Miller does not like the idea of any animals indoors. When he's through with them at the end of the day, he thinks they should be left where they belong; the cows in the cowshed, the goats in the goatshed, the hens in the henhouse, the horse in his stall and the cats wherever they please, as long as that isn't in the house.

'Please, Dad.'

'Sorry, Sophie.'

'It's not fair.'

Mr Miller stands firm. 'That's as maybe, but that's how it is.' Then, more kindly: 'I don't say you'll not be all over it while it's a kitten, but what happens when it grows into a cat? It won't be Sophie's cat then. It will be the Millers' cat.'

'That's not true,' Sophie protests. 'I'll always love it.' She peers at her parents. 'You still love me even though I'm not a baby any more, don't you?'

'Of course we do,' her mother exclaims. 'We'll always love you, even if you *are* shooting up like a weed.'

'And I'll always love my kitten, even when it's a cat.'

Her father stands up. 'Point taken.'

'Then I can have one?'

'I didn't say that.' He looks out of the window. The rain has stopped. A mellow afternoon sun, peeking through a break in the cloud, floods the kitchen with a golden light. 'Might as well see to the animals now the rain's let up,' he says, adding prophetically, 'It's bound to pour again before long.'

Sophie, with chores of her own to see to, follows him out. The kitten is not mentioned again.

'Oh, well,' Sophie tells herself wryly, 'like Kid says, miracles are hard to come by. They haven't exactly beaten a path to the door so far – not when it comes to a kitten for me, anyway.'

Sophie's share of work on the farm is to care for the smaller animals: the goats, Millie and Frieda; Romeo the Rooster and his many wives; and the geese, Murray and Cleo; then there's the old carthorse, Simon, too old for work now but allowed to live out his days where he laboured all his life; and, last but not least, the four barncats. There's Benny, half of him white and half of him black, looking like two cats in one; Max, a handsome tortoiseshell with white paws; Yoghurt (so called because his head got stuck in a pot of yoghurt when he was just a kitten), ginger with a dazzling white 'vest'; and Snowflake, white all over, as her name suggests. Of all the animals, Sophie loves the cats most.

She begins by milking the goats, a job she likes. Crouching between them she puts her pail first under one, then under the other. Their udders have a smooth, rubbery feel, like the bare patch on top of Grandfather Ned's head. (Her other grandfather still has a good head of hair on him.) When there's no more milk to be had, Sophie takes the full pail over to where the four cats have their home and pours some of the still-warm milk into their bowls.

Benny, Max and Yoghurt run up and begin to lap up the milk even as she's pouring it, but though she waits, there's no sign of Snowflake. Sophie puts down the pail and tiptoes to the far corner of the shed, where Snowflake has made her nest. There's nothing there. No kittens, no Snowflake, nothing. The hollow in the hay where the kittens had lain as recently as this morning is cold and empty.

'She's moved them,' Sophie says out loud. 'Something must have frightened her.' Then, 'I wonder where she can have taken them.'

5

Sophie carries the milk to the kitchen, then goes back out to see to the rest of the animals. She scatters corn for the chickens, fills the trough with oats for Simon and puts an old tin plate piled high with apple peelings down for the geese. That done, she returns to the goatshed to feed Millie and Frieda, and to see whether the smell of milk might have lured the white cat back. It hasn't. No watchful green eyes stare back at her from the darkness, no deep growls warn her against coming too close. Snowflake and her kittens really are gone!

'Lost your sheep and don't know where to find them?' her father teases her at supper.

'It's Snowflake, Dad. She's gone!'

'Gone? How do you mean, gone?'

'She's not in the shed with Millie and Frieda and the other cats.'

'She's probably only stretching her legs. She'll soon be back. Bound to with a litter to care for.'

'But that's just it, Dad. She's taken the little ones with her. Every single one.'

'I've never known her to leave the farm with young

ones before,' her father replies, clearly puzzled.

'Could be she felt threatened with three toms around,' her mother puts in.

'Benny, Max and Yoghurt wouldn't hurt Snowflake's children,' Sophie cries indignantly.

'One can never tell with toms, baby. Some times it seems they don't care at all; other times it can get their backs up something terrible.'

'Where do you think she's taken them?'

'Hard to say. Could be anywhere. Plenty of abandoned burrows and warrens out there, and if not there, then maybe she's found a hollow tree, a dense hedge, a farm with no other cats though I don't suppose there are many of those hereabouts.'

'*Farmer* Stone hasn't got any cats up at his place,' Sophie says. She looks at her parents, her eyes dark with fear. 'If she has gone there, he'll kill her. I know he will.'

'Whatever notions you may have about *Farmer* Stone, he would not shoot an animal with young,' her father says with conviction.

'He would, Dad! He's all bad.'

'That will do, Sophie!'

'But, Dad.'

'Stop nagging me about Snowflake, girl. She knows how to take care of herself . . . and her kittens.'

'But . . .'

'No, Sophie. You are letting your imagination run away with you. I won't have it.'

Sophie shoots up from her chair, storms out of the kitchen and into her room. She gets into her nightdress, throws herself into bed and pulls the covers over her head. Boy, is she mad!

Later, still awake and smouldering, she hears her mother come into her room. Sophie doesn't move. She pretends to be asleep.

'Goodnight, pet,' Mrs Miller says, addressing the round bump in the middle of the bed. 'I hope you remembered to brush your teeth before going to bed.'

The bump heaves. It slides to the floor. Face tight, eyes staring stubbornly ahead, it marches to the bathroom, returns – a little toothpaste clinging to the corners of its mouth – and, still looking neither left nor right, dives back under the covers to its warm, cosy den in the centre of the bed.

'Good-night, then,' Mrs Miller calls out softly.

Sophie doesn't reply. There's a lump of ice where her heart should be. Her mother goes out, closing the door behind her. For ages afterwards Sophie, curled up in her snug burrow, wishes her mother were back so she could say good-night to her. But it's too late. Her mother and father have long since gone to bed themselves. Instead Sophie, who feels she won't be able to sleep unless she says good-night to someone, addresses the missing cat. 'Come back, Snowflake,' she whispers, 'come back soon.'

Moments later she's asleep and the rain, which has held off all evening, begins to drum against her window, accompanied by the thin whine of a rapidly rising wind.

6

In the deep hours of this dark, stormy night Sophie, tossing and turning in troubled sleep, hears a cry. Immediately she is awake. There it is again. She turns her head to the sound. It's coming from outside, from beyond the walls of her room. Urgent, insistent, the weary, hopeless cry of someone, something, sensing that time is running out.

Then it stops, only to start again moments later more frantic than before, cutting through the mad lullaby of the wind and the rain and the fog in her head.

She throws aside the bedclothes and before she knows it she's racing across to the french windows, throwing them open and running out to stand knee-deep in the wind-whipped, rain-soaked grass, indifferent to the savage fury of the storm, the hollow sound of thunder. Suddenly a light is switched on behind her.

'Sophie! Get back in. At once.'

Her parents roused from their sleep by the wind howling at the doors and windows of the cottage and now swirling through the house like a dervish, can hardly believe their eyes. What is the child doing outside in the rain?

Sophie hears them but doesn't move. Her father, and mother, macs thrown over their nightwear rush at her and, each grabbing an arm, attempt to pull her inside.

'Let me go,' Sophie shouts, 'let me go . . . Mum . . . Dad . . . Listen . . . please . . . please . . . listen.'

'Now look here,' her father commands, his voice swollen with authority.

'Listen,' Sophie pleads, tears and rain pouring down her face.

And this time they do and soon they hear it too, the sad, weary cry so weak and forlorn in all that open air. Sophie's father gives a low whistle. 'A cat,' he says, 'I'll eat my hat if that's not a cat out there.'

'It's Snowflake, Dad,' Sophie says, her voice tense with anxiety. 'It's Snowflake. I know it is, and she's hurt, I can hear it.'

A bedraggled, sorry-looking white cat, its fur sticking to its body, something black hanging from its mouth, limps into the patch of warm, yellow light streaming out of the open door. 'Snowflake, Snowflake, you've come back, you've come back,' Sophie cries, clapping her hands together. 'I knew you would . . . Oh, I just knew you would.' Her heart beating wildly, she sinks to her knees beside the white cat, ready to hug her, hold her tight, make sure she never goes away again. But before she can do so, Snowflake opens her jaws and lets drop the thing she's carrying. It falls into the tall, wet grass with a soft thud. Without thinking, Sophie gets her hand under it and scoops it up. To her amazement and delight she sees that it is a tiny kitten and, though it seems more dead than alive right now, Sophie's heart turns a somersault and her stomach fills with butterflies. A kitten! A kitten! For her? 'Snowflake,' she whispers, 'is this your child? Is it for me? Are you giving it to me?'

The white cat lifts her eyes. She shuts them, opens them, shuts them . . . once . . . twice . . . three times. Then her head suddenly falls forward as if she can no longer summon the strength to hold it up. There is a trickle of blood from her mouth. The rain keeps washing it away but it comes back again and again. Sophie stares at it, wondering in a dazed kind of way how this can be. And at last she understands. Her eyes fill with hot, scalding tears. Poor, poor Snowflake . . . poor white cat. Snowflake, her sea-green eyes beginning to cloud over, blinks one more time and is still.

Sophie, feeling her heart is about to break, stares and stares. She can't, doesn't want to, believe the white cat will never move again. It's like a bad dream, a horrible, horrible nightmare. Slowly she gets up. Hugging the kitten to her, she watches her father dig a hole and bury the white cat.

'I won't be able to sleep knowing she's all alone out here,' she sobs as the last spadeful of earth is patted down.

'Snowflake doesn't mind where she is now,' her father tells her gently. 'There's nothing any of us can do for her now, but we can do something for her child. Bet it can do with a drop or two of warm milk.'

Sophie turns away from the sad-looking little

mound of earth and allows herself to be led indoors. Her father is right. It is Snowflake's child who needs her now. In the kitchen, Sophie drips warmed milk on to the kitten's lips and nose, hoping it will lick them off. But Snowflake's child is either too frightened or too tired or both to want even to try. Instead the tiny, frail bundle gives them all a resigned look out of its kitten-blue eyes and, curling itself into a tight ball, opts for sleep. Sophie looks questioningly at her parents – especially her dad.

'It's all right, you may keep it,' he says, anticipating her question. He is immediately rewarded by a brilliant smile.

'Thanks, Dad,' Sophie whispers, all choked up.

So, from having been steeped in sorrow, she is now awash with happiness because there's a kitten nestling in the crook of her arm – just like she's always wanted.

7

At daybreak Snowflake's child, who has spent the first night in its new home nestled in Sophie's hair, opens its eyes, yawns, stretches and begins to look around for its mother. It starts to call her, low at first but when that fails, at full volume, sending out wave after wave of piercing cries impossible to ignore however sleepy one might be.

Sophie opens first one eye, then the other. The yowling stops. The little cat clambers on to her chest and just sits there, front legs straight and close together, paws neatly side by side, tail politely curled round – a wee King of the Castle come to rouse the kitchen staff.

Taken aback at seeing the kitten's face so close to her own, Sophie blinks. The kitten equally startled by the sudden movement, shoots up and back in one movement. Then, curiosity getting the better of it, it cranes its scraggy neck forward, puts out a paw and gives the fluttering eyelids a cautious pat. Sophie giggles and squeezes them more tightly together. Coal-black puss now sets to patting not just the eyelids but the whole face, soft, gentle, light-as-air pats. Next, a minute tongue, rough as a cheese grater, goes to work on her cheeks. Sophie looks up and wipes her face with a corner of the sheet but still she does not get up. The little animal, its tum hollow as a drum and desperate for something to fill it with, resorts to new tactics. Darting forward, it smartly nips the tip of her nose and, in case that's not enough, goes on to sink its sharp little teeth into the point of her chin.

'Ouch! You little brute!' Sophie shouts. She sits up, swings her legs over the side of the bed and pushes her feet into a pair of slippers. Pulling on her dressing-gown, she gently drops the kitten into one of the pockets. 'Should keep you out of mischief while I get on with things,' she tells it. 'Well, I suppose I'd better get something down you on the double or you'll soon have everyone awake with your yowling.'

Snowflake's child, finding this new nest to its liking, settles down in it to await breakfast. It looks up at Sophie with sky-blue eyes, round as buttons. 'Mischief?' It seems to be saying. 'Mischief? What, me? As if I would!'

Sophie has just taken the pan off the flame when the kitchen door opens and her mother comes in. 'Good-morning, pet,' Mrs Miller yawns. 'Didn't expect to run into you this early on a Saturday morning.'

Sophie points to her pocket. 'The kitten made such a racket I just had to get up,' she explains. Mrs Miller peeks down at it.

'A fine place. A very fine place indeed for a little cat,' she agrees.

'Thought it would stop it from running about. Anyway, it seems to like it there.'

'Let's take a look at it, then.'

Sophie carefully lowers her hand into her pocket, cups it round the kitten and lifts it out.

'Goodness, aren't you just adorable?' Sophie's mother coos. The scrap gives her a startled look and shrinks into the hollow of Sophie's hand. 'And how are we after our great adventure, then?' Mrs Miller goes on. 'No lasting ill effects, I hope.' She puts out her hand to stroke it, but the kitten will have none of this. Hissing, clawing and spitting, it backs off, eyes narrowed, whiskers twitching, ears flat against the head, a ridge of hair rising along its spine. 'Well, I'm blowed, the little rag-bag is all teeth and claws,' Mrs Miller laughs.

Sophie, who has been pouring milk into a saucer, looks up. 'Say that again, Mum.'

'I said the little rag-bag is all teeth and claws.'

'Teeth and claws,' Sophie repeats, 'would make a good name for it, don't you think, Mum?'

'Better find out whether it is a boy or a girl before you name it,' her mother advises.

Sophie turns the kitten over on its back while her mother holds its tail aside. 'It's a boy!' Sophie shouts. Her mother agrees. The squirming kitten is put back on to its feet. 'Snowflake's child,' Sophie says solemnly, 'I now name you, Teeth . . . no, Tooth and – Claw.'

The kitten, indifferent to the importance of the moment, glares, growls, spits and just looks generally put out. To smooth things over Sophie sets him down in front of the saucer of milk. To her surprise he doesn't begin to drink at once, as she expects. He sniffs it, puts a paw into it, raises it to his mouth, smells it, sinks the other paw into it, holds it up to his nose, has another sniff, does a little dance round the saucer (leaving a ring of tiny white paw prints on the lino), then, satisfied at last, lowers his head, sticks out his tongue and attempts to lap up the milk. As far as first tries go, it's not bad: he splutters, chokes, coughs and wheezes until it looks like there's more milk on him than in him.

The whole pathetic performance has Sophie and her mother in stitches. They laugh so much that their sides ache. 'Think he's getting any of it, Mum?' Sophie manages to squeeze out at last. Her mother, shaking with merriment, nods. And he must have done, because all of a sudden he stops drinking, runs his little pink tongue round his mouth, stretches and then flops on to the floor. Curled up, nose to tail, he is out for the count, KO'd by Millie's and Frieda's milk!

'A contented customer, I'd say,' Mrs Miller hiccups, wiping tears of laughter from her eyes.

Sophie looks tenderly at her small charge. 'It'll be great when he's grown a little. We'll do lots and lots of things together then,' she says happily. She looks up at her mother. 'Last night really happened, didn't it, Mum?'

Her mother strokes her hair. 'It certainly did, pet. Your kitten's no dream and if anyone should dare to doubt you, you've got him right here to prove it.'

8

'Mum, wouldn't it be lovely if Tooth and Claw's eyes were to stay blue?' Sophie says wistfully.

'Black cats with blue eyes are very rare,' her mother replies. 'Anyway, aren't black cats with blue eyes supposed to be witches' cats?'

'Wouldn't it be fun if Tooth and Claw turned out to be a magic cat. Think of all the tricks you could play on people,' Sophie giggles.

Her dad looks up. 'Bit of a mouthful, isn't it?' he says.

Sophie looks at him wide-eyed. 'Being a magic cat?'

He laughs. 'No, silly. I mean isn't the name you've given him something of a mouthful?'

Sophie scratches the back of her head. 'You think so? Well, how about . . .' She thinks for a while, then she has it: 'TC! How about TC?'

'That's better. Tooth and Claw sounds rather too fierce for such a little fellow.'

'He is fierce,' Sophie returns proudly.

'He'll make a fine tom,' her mother says, 'a really fine mouser. Got that kind of look about him.'

'You can tell, can you?' Mr Miller teases his wife.

'I can at that,' she replies haughtily.

'Don't mind him going for mice and rats, but I hope he'll leave the birds alone,' Sophie sighs. 'I hate it when cats kill birds.'

'It's the way of cats, pet,' her mother says. 'Nature often seems hard, but on the whole it knows what it's doing.'

'Balance,' her father booms. 'There must be balance in nature or the world will collapse on itself like a pack of cards.'

'I know, Dad, but I still hope he won't get too many.'

'Only those careless enough to come within his reach,' he laughs.

'Will he catch birds even if he's really well fed?'

'Being well fed has nothing to do with it. A cat is a born hunter. A full belly wouldn't stop Benny, Max or Yoghurt trying their luck on some ill-fated sparrow, would it?'

'But that's because they're wild,' Sophie protests. 'TC will grow up tame.'

'There's no such thing as a tame cat, honey. At heart all cats are wild.'

'Not TC. He'll be a house cat.'

'A model puss,' her mother giggles.

'A proper gentleman,' her father guffaws.

'Files his claws and trims his whiskers.'

'Brushes his coat.'

'Washes behind the ears.'

'Comes to the table dressed in top hat and tails.'

'Never dips a paw in the cream when no one's looking.'

'Doesn't gobble his food.'

'Never speaks with his mouth full.'
'Doesn't speak unless spoken to.'
'Is seen but not heard.'
Sophie stares at her parents as if seeing them for the first time. 'Oh, you . . .', she bursts out, then flees to her room to get out of the way of more teasing, wondering how grown-up people can be so silly.

TC sleeps . . . and sleeps . . . and sleeps. Every so often he wakes up, takes some more milk, polishes his whiskers, yawns, stretches, then goes to sleep again . . . and so it goes on.
'I wish TC would stay awake for more than just a few minutes at a time,' Sophie complains to her mother.
'You must give him a chance to catch up on lost sleep,' her mother answers. 'It's anyone's guess how long it took poor Snowflake to bring him here.'
Sophie too can't help wondering how far the white cat had had to come with her tiny burden – in pain, dying, knowing only that she must keep going till she reaches her destination, the place instinct tells her her child will be safe. All at once Sophie remembers the trickle of blood that had run out of the corner of Snowflake's mouth. She gasps. Of course! She's amazed at herself for not having thought of it earlier!
'Mum,' she says, looking at her mother with dark, troubled eyes. 'I think I know where Snowflake went after she left us.'
'Where, pet?'
'To Farmer Stone's place. That's where,' Sophie replies grimly.

'How do you make that out?'

'Didn't you see the blood on her? She'd been shot at, and no one else around here would shoot a cat except that ogre.'

'Sophie!'

She gives her parents a hard stare. 'I don't care what you say. He did it. He shot Snowflake, and the rest of her litter too I shouldn't wonder.'

'I know it's what you're thinking, but let's not be too hasty about Farmer Stone,' her father says. 'I grant you he appears to be a hard man, but it would take a heartless one to shoot a cat with young.'

'Well, that's just what he is,' Sophie exclaims. 'He's bad and mean and . . .' Too full of tears to go on, she runs to her room to cry.

In the kitchen her parents regard one another across the table. 'What do you think?' Mrs Miller asks her husband.

'I don't know,' he says. 'Perhaps Sophie's right. Could be, that man is all flint . . .'

9

Monday can't come quickly enough for Sophie. All through Saturday and Sunday she prays Kid will find a way to come over to see her, but it's no use. And she so wants to show him her kitten! Still, there's nothing for it but to swallow her impatience and wait till they meet up for school on Monday morning. From past experience she knows it is no good her going to see him. Mr and Mrs Brown have made plain their ideas about how weekends should be spent. As Kid says, she (Sophie) knows what they are like. It makes Sophie angry just thinking about them. She wishes they wouldn't treat Kid like a farm-hand. No, worse. A farm-hand at least has one day off to look forward to!

Left to herself Sophie can't help wondering what Kid will say when she tells him about TC. How should she put it? Should she come straight out with it – 'You'll never believe it but I've got a kitten', or, 'Guess what happened Friday night?', or 'I've got something to show you'?

And Kid will look at her and smile that little crooked smile of his which makes it seem as if he's not sure whether she's on the level or not, and ask in

a slow drawl that's all Kid: 'What?'
'It's very tiny and all black and furry.'
'A pet tarantula.'
'Nope.'
'A black rabbit?'
'Wrong again.'
Then at last the penny will drop. 'A kitten, you've got a kitten!' Sophie will nod and beam and say, 'That's right, a kitten. A little cat all my own', and go on to tell him the whole story.

Monday morning she's up early. She gives TC his milk, spends a while playing with him before getting washed and dressed and is all ready to go when her mother comes down. 'Bye, Mum,' she shouts.
Mrs Miller looks at her watch. 'A little early, aren't you? It's only just eight o'clock.'
'I know,' Sophie answers impatiently, 'but I've got so much to tell Kid.'
'I'm sure he won't be standing by the gate this early,' her mother says. 'Now how about coming with me to the kitchen for a spot of breakfast?'
'Don't want any,' Sophie says, peeved at having had the wind taken out of her sails.
'Breakfast!' Mrs Miller says firmly.
'But I'm not hungry. Why do I have to have breakfast if I'm not hungry?'
'To stop your tummy from rumbling in class,' Mrs Miller replies calmly.
There's nothing for it but to follow her mother into the kitchen. When at last the porridge is put down in front of her, Sophie, who has spent the time so far

playing with TC, now hands the cat to her mother. She begins to gulp down the porridge in large spoonfuls, but it is still so hot it makes her eyes smart. Half-way through, she shoots up from her chair, gives TC a quick kiss, asks her mother if she'll keep an eye on him till after school and bolts out of the house before anyone can call her back.

Once out on the road she sets off towards Kid's house at a gallop, not stopping till she's in sight of his gate. But he's not there! She waits. Perhaps she's still too early. Oh that porridge . . . she's late, that's what it is! She promised Kid she'd be on time and now he's gone without her. Taking a deep breath, she begins to run again, finally catching up with Kid at the bottom of the lane, about to cross the main road to the school.

'Kid,' she pants, 'I'm sorry I'm late but . . . but you'll never guess what has happened. Snowflake brought me one of her kittens, only Stone shot her and . . .'

Kid, who happens to have got out of bed on the wrong side this morning, does not want to know. 'Cats,' he yells at her. 'Cats, cats, cats. That's all you can talk about. Well, I'm sick of hearing about cats. Now, leave me alone.' He pats Smith sharply on the rump and orders him back up the lane. Then he strides across the road and, once on the other side, breaks into a run.

Sophie, knowing that is no way to cross a main road – or any road for that matter – follows blindly, but Kid is a much faster runner and she has a job keeping up with him. 'Kid', she pleads. 'Kid, wait!'

This only makes Kid run faster. Sophie slows down to a walk, her eyes hot with tears. 'It's not fair. Nothing ever goes the way you plan,' she thinks bitterly.

The rest of the day is awful too. Kid doesn't so much as look at her. When school's out in the afternoon he goes on the bus with the others, leaving her to climb the lane alone. She bites the inside of her mouth to keep herself from crying and drags her feet as if she's pulling on a ball and chain. Home at last, she makes straight for her room. TC will cheer her up. But though she looks for him in every nook and cranny, she can't find him. Downcast, she goes to the shed to ask her mother if she knows where he is.

'Mum, have you seen TC?' she asks.

'Last I checked on him he was on your bed, fast asleep,' her mother replies. She is too busy measuring a piece of wood to look up.

'Well, he's not there now,' Sophie says rudely, deliberately thrusting her foot into a pile of wood shavings, scattering them all over the floor. 'You could have kept an eye on him. It'll be your fault if anything's happened to him!'

At this her mother does look up. 'That will do, young lady.' From her tone, Sophie knows she won't take kindly to any talkback.

Sophie, thinking her mother the most heartless person in the world, storms out of the shed and right into the arms of her father. 'Dad, dad!' she cries, 'TC's gone. I've looked all over for him but I can't find him.'

'Her father, who's just finished mucking out

Simon's stall, leans his pitchfork against the wall, wipes his hands on his dungarees and, taking her by the hand, leads her across the yard in the direction of the goatshed. 'Don't take on so, girl,' he says. 'I'll show you where your kitten is.'

He's as good as his word. Close to Millie's and Frieda's shed, in a patch of sunlit ground, the little black cat is quietly washing itself.

Sophie blinks away the tears. 'Thanks, Dad.'

He ruffles her hair and the two of them, held by the charm of the scene, stay to watch the antics of the little cat. He's surprisingly thorough for such a young animal: mouth, nose, eyes, whiskers, head, ears, behind the ears, between the toes, front paws, back paws, tail. Spit and polish, spit and polish, on and on until all of him shines like polished coal. Satisfied at last, he yawns, rolls into a fluffy ball, curls his tail about him, and taking no notice of his human audience, nods off in the sunshine. A little way away three fierce-looking toms watch the proceedings with interest. Sophie points to them. 'They won't hurt him, will they, Dad?'

'I doubt it or they would have gone for him by now.'

Sophie lets out a sigh of relief. 'Phew! Am I glad.'

'I expect you are.'

'You would be too if it was your cat.'

'True. Anyway I'm sure they'll make friends with him. He is too small to be a threat to them. If they really take to him they might teach him all the things his mother would have taught him.'

'You mean hunting and things?'

'Yes, that, and something as important.'

'What?'

'To recognize danger.'

'Good! Then perhaps he'll keep clear of Stone and his murderous dog.'

Her father laughs. 'One day you might discover that the murderous dog is the gentlest hound that ever roamed these parts.'

'Fat chance!'

10

The next morning Sophie, who has hardly slept a wink all night for worrying about how things will go between herself and Kid today, sails past his gate, nose and chin in the air. And now it is Kid who runs after her and, on catching her up, tells her he's sorry he was so horrible the day before. Sophie immediately lowers her nose and soon she is telling Kid about Snowflake and TC, and Kid says it's a shame about Snowflake but that at least she has a cat of her own at long last. When Sophie tells him what she's calling the kitten, Kid says, 'Yeah, it's a swell name.' At any rate he doesn't know of any other cat with that name. 'Wait till I tell the others,' Sophie cries happily. (She means the rest of the gang.)

'You mean you haven't yet?' Kid exclaims. Knowing how she feels about cats, especially now she has one of her own, he expects her to have spread the news round the world by now.

'I wanted to yesterday but I guess I was too miserable then,' Sophie says carefully. She doesn't want Kid to think she is fishing for him to apologize further.

But perhaps it is what he has in mind to do anyway

because he at once replies: 'I acted like a pig, all right.'

'Oh, let's forget it! It's history now,' Sophie responds.

'OK,' Kid agrees.

And now that they have squared things with one another the two old friends set off down the lane at full pelt, Smith beside them beating the air with his tail and yelping like a puppy.

They reach the school just as the rest of the 'lane kids', Titch, Sprat, Busker, The Squire, little Idira and Archie Williams are getting off the school bus. Kid and Sophie wait till everyone is out and together they troop into the playground and, while they wait for the bell to go Sophie tells them all about the events of the weekend.

'How come you didn't say anything yesterday?' Charlie asks when she has finished.

'That's a long story,' Sophie says glancing meaningfully at Kid.

'What's this about yesterday. Anything happened I should know about?' Archie says. As usual he has not been paying attention. While Sophie has been talking he has busied himself making life difficult for the column of ants passing between his feet. Consequently he has missed much of the story.

'Too late, fat-head. You should have been listening, shouldn't you?' Busker says giving him a playful shove.

'Come on you freaks, give a guy a break,' Archie pleads.

Sophie willingly goes over the story once again, just for him.

'You mean your dad is letting you have an animal in

the house after all?' Archie says.

'Right,' Sophie assures him, 'and what's more, now it has happened he feels really good about it.'

A wicked glint comes into Archie's eyes. 'You just wait till it begins to shred the curtains and sharpen its claws on the furniture,' he warns her.

'It won't,' Sophie answers instantly springing to the defence of her little pet.

'It will and then your mum and dad are going to wish they'd given you a stuffed one instead,' Archie says with glee.

'Trust you to turn a nice story like that into blood and guts,' The Squire says disdainfully.

'No need for you to bust yours, Squire,' Archie retorts, 'anyway I was only kidding.'

And really everyone is pleased for Sophie. Even Archie though he likes to pretend otherwise.

Now that everything is right with the world again, after school Sophie asks Kid if he would like to come home with her to see her cat.

'Great,' Kid says, 'but I'd better ask my mum first.'

'Don't be long,' she calls out and begins to swing on the Browns' gate to pass the time.

Kid shoots up the drive, Smith, as always at his heels. He makes straight for the kitchen, where he knows his mother will be busy packing eggs at this time of the day. Normally Kid helps her with it when he comes back from school, but today he would like to see Sophie's cat.

'Mum, can I go with Sophie to see her new kitten, can I?' he asks, stumbling over the words.

'So, Sophie Miller has got her cat, then,' Mrs Brown

says, her eyes on the pyramid of eggs in front of her.

'Yes. Can I go? Can I?'

'All right, then,' Mrs Brown agrees reluctantly. 'But you are not to stay, hear. There are all these eggs to deliver when your dad gets home and you have got to go with him and give him a hand. I can't. I've got enough to do as it is. Always thinking of yourself, you are.'

'Yes, Mum. Thanks, Mum.'

Kid is out of the kitchen before his mother can change her mind. Smith, however, is less fortunate. He is about to follow his master when a command to 'Stay' nails him to the spot. 'Oh no, my precious. One of you skiving's bad enough. Now you just be a good dog and go round up the chickens for me.' Smith looks at her imploringly out of his big, moist eyes. 'No good you looking at me like that, you crafty hound,' Mrs Brown tells him hard heartedly.

Smith drags himself towards the door, his beautiful golden tail brushing the floor. 'Woof, woof,' he tries. Mrs Brown lifts an egg and pretends to throw it at him. 'Out! on the double!' Smith knows when he's beaten. Throwing her one last dejected look he goes, ears drooping, tail limp, to earn his keep. 'A dog's life and no mistake,' he seems to be saying, and, 'Dog's best friend! Come again, come again!'

'Phew,' Kid exclaims when he's with Sophie again.

'What's the matter?'

'Nothing, really. Just Mum's in one of her I-can't-do-everything moods. Boy, is she hard to take when it comes over her!'

'I know what you mean,' Sophie says. 'Mine's like that sometimes, and Dad too. It's not so bad when it's only one of them, but when it hits both of them together . . . Whoa!'

'I'll not be like that with my children,' Kid vows.

'Me neither.'

They walk on in silence, each trying to figure out how it is that parents are so hard to understand at times.

11

Black cat on my lap,
What do you dream of?
Sprats at dawn,
Sprats at dusk,
Sprats for breakfast,
Sprats for lunch!

They find TC asleep on Sophie's bed, curled up like a plump caterpillar on her pillow, chin on paws, rat-like tail thrown about him, a sliver of ice-cream-pink tongue sticking out between tiny white teeth.

'He's a prize,' Kid whispers, then asks, 'Where does he sleep at night?'

'Right here of course.'

'You're lucky. Smith isn't even allowed in the house after dark. I've asked Dad if I could have him sleeping at the end of my bed, but he said no. He says Smith is a guard dog, not a lap-dog.'

'Couldn't you smuggle him in after your folks have gone to bed?'

'You crazy? Dad would kill me if he found out!'

Sophie is sorry for Kid. His dad is always so hard on him. 'Must be hard having a copper for a dad,' she says sympathetically.

'Yeah. Especially one who thinks he's on duty all the time. He never lets up. Treats me like I was on probation or something.' He looks at her darkly, his blue eyes shooting sparks. 'Some day I'll just run off. That'll show him.'

'Kid Brown,' Sophie replies. 'If you do, I want to be in on it. Swear you'll not go without me.'

'All right.'

Just then TC opens his eyes. He looks at the children, stretches, yawns widely and makes his way unsteadily towards Sophie. She at once notices something different about him. It's his eyes. They are no longer all blue: flecks of green can just be seen in the corners.

'Look,' she tells Kid. 'Look, his eyes are changing colour.'

'It's like they've been splashed with green paint,' Kid remarks.

'Would have been nice if they'd stayed blue, but green is fine too. Snowflake's eyes were green. I expect he takes after her. Still, I did fancy the idea of him being a witch's cat.'

'Just think. We could have asked him to turn Stone into a puddle,' Kid points out.

'Have him liquefied and jump into him,' Sophie goes on with relish.

Kid puts out a finger and gently rubs TC under the chin. The little black cat at once begins to purr. 'Sounds just like The Squire's Rolls,' Kid laughs.

Sophie hands him the kitten. Kid takes it and holds it as if it's made of glass. 'Go on, hold him properly.

He won't break, you know,' she assures him.

Kid holds TC up to his face, his cheek against the soft fur of the little animal. 'He's so tiny. When Smith was a pup, he was ten times bigger.' He gives him back to Sophie. 'Got yourself a real tiger there, all right.'

'Yup,' says Sophie, all but bursting with pride.

'You better look sharp or he'll soon be winding you round his little finger – well, paw anyway,' Kid warns her.

'Don't mind if he does. I tell you now, this here kitten is going to be the most pampered quadruped in the land.'

'Huh?'

'Quadruped. Anything walking about on four legs is a quadruped.'

'What's something on two pins, then?'

'A biped, of course.'

'Of course,' Kid mimics, the colour rushing to his face. 'Swallowed a *Thesaurus*, have we?'

'Sorry. I didn't mean to show off. Honest.'

Kid casts a glance at the many books fighting for space on Sophie's shelves. 'It's OK. Reckon it's keeping your nose in them books does it.'

A mischievous smile begins to play on Sophie's lips. So, Kid thinks her a bookworm, does he? Well, she might be one at that, but she'll show him being a bookworm is not all work and no play! She puts TC down on her pillow and, before Kid knows what is happening, she grabs him by the arm and breaks into a wild dance, chanting at the top of her voice:

'Now TC's here I'm smitten, bitten,
Books will lie unread and homework unwritten,
All day long I'll play with my kitten!'

'Lay off, will ya,' Kid shouts.

But there's no stopping Sophie now. On and on she rushes, spinning round and round the room like a top, with Kid in tow.

'Stop! Cool it! No need to go at a million miles an hour,' Kid cries.

Sophie, taking not the slightest notice, treats this as her cue for more:

'Million, Billion, Jillion,
Trillion, zillion.
We'll ride a tourbillion,
Rob a postilion,
Sip tea in a pavilion,
And all cosmopolitan,
We'll go home on the Metropolitan!'

'You're crazy!'

'Crazy, mazy, upsy-daisy . . .'

'Let go of me. I'm getting all giddy!'

'Giddy, biddy, middy, Zebedeee,' Sophie hollers, louder and louder, until her mother, alarmed by all the noise, rushes in and demands to know what is going on.

'Nothing, Mum' Sophie burbles.

'Didn't sound like nothing to me.'

'We were just making up rhymes, Mum.'

'Sounds more like a party at the asylum,' Mrs Miller snorts. 'Now, if you are going to sing, or make up rhymes, or whatever, please do it in a more civilized manner.'

'Yes, Mum,' Sophie hoots, her voice oozing mischief.

'I mean it,' her mother warns her.

'Yes, Mum,' Sophie says, bubbling like a brook inside.

'You're a right nutter you are,' Kid roars when Mrs Miller has gone.

'Nutter, butter, gutter.' This is all it takes to set them off again. Soon their shrieks are fit to bring the walls tumbling down. They certainly bring Mrs Miller back a second time.

'What's got into you two today?' she thunders at them. 'Break it up. Right now.'

'Sorry,' Sophie splutters, wondering how many more times she'll have to apologize for laughing before the day is out.

'I'd better go. Got to help Dad deliver the eggs,' Kid says.

'See you tomorrow,' Sophie answers.

'Thanks for letting me see the kitten. He's great.'

'Thanks.'

'Cheers, then. Goodbye, Mrs Miller.'

'Goodbye, Kid. Sophie, see Kid out.'

'Yes, Mum.'

The two go, one behind the other, hardly able to hold back the waves of laughter rising and falling in their throats.

'Sophie Miller, you're nuts,' Kid bursts out as soon as they are out of earshot of Mrs Miller.

'Nuts, mutts, smuts, doughnuts, chestnuts, butter-nuts,' Sophie giggles.

'Catgut,' Kid adds wickedly.

'Hey, Kid!'

'What?'

'You just rhymed.'

Kid stares at her. Suddenly his eyes go very bright as if he's done something special. 'Yeah, I have, haven't I?' he chuckles, and he thrust his hands into his pockets, not knowing what else to do with them.

12

June, July. At last the day comes when there's no more school. Not for weeks and weeks! At last Sophie can get her fill of TC. They are together every day throughout the summer. TC becomes as good at following her about as Smith is with Kid. The four of them often go for long hikes over the fields or in the woods bordering Upper Catsfield, the animals ahead, Sophie and Kid following behind, socks and shoes off to give their feet an airing.

On really fine days they take a picnic along: something to drink, hardboiled eggs, crisps, apples, cheese and Marmite sandwiches and whatever else is on offer at home. Sophie always shares hers with TC. Thanks to her, he has come to prefer 'human' fare to tinned stuff, which he will only eat when there is nothing else to be had. And this in spite of the fact that Sophie's mother buys nothing but Kitty-Bites for him, the very best in cat food as advertised on TV by haughty Siamese, choosy Burmese and other upper-crust moggies. It does not impress the black cat. Sauntering up to his dish, he will knock it over, turn his back on it and scratch imaginary 'dirt' over it. Then, throwing the unappetizing mess an insolent look, he will walk away, head high, tail proudly erect. Aristocats can eat the stuff as much as they like. For his part he is content to settle for whatever is on Sophie's plate – or anyone else's come to that.

Sophie thinks it funny but Kid warns her that habits like this could turn TC into a thief. Sophie says she can't see how the occasional treat off her plate will do that. Kid insists she is making a rod for her own back. If TC can't have what he wants, he's bound to end up stealing it. Sophie, laughing this off, assures him he's exaggerating.

'Bet you a copy of *Soccer Heroes* he'll strike before summer's up,' Kid says – *Soccer Heroes* is his favourite comic.

Sophie takes up the bet. They shake hands on it with Smith and TC acting as witnesses.

On these hikes it must be said that Smith is by far the better behaved of the two animals. Kid has only to command and he'll obey. Not so TC. He doesn't make his way in an orderly fashion like Smith. Oh no! He is all over the place. Here, there, everywhere: chasing butterflies, stalking grasshoppers, meting out playful blows to buttercups and daisies, shooting like a black arrow through the fields of rape and vanishing into burrows, hollows, under rocks, in thickets and up trees too high for him to make it down again unaided. Sophie has had to come to his rescue plenty of times. So, while Kid and Smith frolic in the grass, paddle in the cool, crystal waters of the stream or just lie stretched out in some sunny glade soaking up the sun, Sophie is darting about shouting

herself hoarse with: 'TC, come here!' or 'TC, where are you?' or, 'Bad puss, don't climb that tree', or 'Don't crawl into that hole', or 'TC, you're a pain, a right nuisance. I'll not take you with me ever again!' and so on.

But of course, she doesn't mean it. It's an empty threat and he knows it. Putting his head on one side, he looks at her in a way designed to soften the most determined heart. 'You are impossible,' Sophie tells him in feigned anger. 'One day that curiosity of yours will land you in big trouble.'

Kid shades his eyes from the blinding summer sun with his arm and looks up at them both through half-closed lids. 'Especially if he happens to have a run-in with a fox,' he says in a doomladened you-just-wait-and-see voice.

Sophie strokes TC's silky whiskers with her finger. 'Not him, he'd never do anything so daft. This is a smart puss!'

13

August arrives with sweltering heat. The high temperatures have Upper Catsfield panting and for once wishing for a cloud or two to appear on the horizon. Everything in sight is drooping: people, trees, flowers, animals. A month of dream weather and the whole country is praying for rain! Apart, that is, from the landlord of The White Cat, who is doing a roaring trade in lagers, and the supermarket proprietor, who is doing equally well with ice-creams and cold drinks. The two gentlemen concerned, Mr King and Mr Leach, rub their hands together and hope the summer will never end. Whatever anyone else thinks, they are doing very nicely, thank you!

Sophie, on her third ice-lolly, is sitting on the step outside her room, the french windows wide open behind her, about to begin a new book. TC is lying in her shade, looking as if he might be going to take a nap, when a sudden movement further up the field catches his attention. He shoots up, ears back, tail bushed, fur bristling, his green eyes mere slits against the white August light, staring fixedly ahead. Sophie, wondering how he can bear to move at all in the heat, follows his stare but, well, there's nothing to see.

Romeo the Rooster is around with his harem, the goats, Millie and Frieda, are somewhere too, as are Simon and, towards the top of the field, barely visible, the two geese, Murray and Cleo, deep in grass and flowers. Sophie can just make out their stubby, quivering tails. So what's the big deal? She returns to her book. She doesn't know it but the fact is that she and TC have been looking at the same thing, only he's a cat and to him feathers in the grass is a sight no self-respecting feline can be expected to ignore. Dropping on to his belly, he begins a slow, careful slither towards the unsuspecting victims, nose to the ground, looking like a fat, furry slug. Curious now, Sophie puts down her book and follows him with her eyes. Try as she might, she can't think what he's after. Not until he's almost on the two geese does she guess. She opens her mouth to warn him but, too late! With a growl from deep down in his throat he launches himself at the two birds. Poor TC. He is no match at all for Murray and Cleo.

In a furious show of alarm and hurt dignity, manifested by the beating of wings and showers of hissed abuse, they set on the hapless kitten with unbridled malice. While Cleo stabs at his head Murray deals out nips to his tail and rump with a view to causing the black cat maximum pain and anguish. The upshot is a most dreadful din, and the effect on the other animals grazing nearby is electric. Soon the field is resounding with chickens cackling, goats bleating, the horse neighing and cats miaowing – Benny, Max and Yoghurt have been drawn to the action and are at the ringside, howling encouragement to TC. The result is a cacophony so hideous that it drives Sophie to stop her ears!

As for TC – whose teeth and claws don't seem to have the slightest effect on the incensed geese – all he wants is OUT. Thoroughly rattled, he tries to escape by running through Cleo's legs. Instead he somehow finds himself first under her, then, somehow, on her back. Startled out of its wits, the terrified goose goes for vertical take-off Harrier-style.

The sudden upward motion throws TC to the ground. Though somewhat stunned by the fall, he doesn't waste any time getting himself together. Within the blinking of an eye, he is scooting back to the house, past the three toms, the chickens, the goats, the old horse and finally Sophie. On familiar ground again – and grateful for it – he dives under her bed, where he lies low for several days nursing his damaged pride and sore tail.

As the summer months roll by TC gains courage through experience. Soon he is a swift and practised hunter, although now he tends to try his luck on smaller prey. As for Murray and Cleo, he is careful to keep his distance from them, even if they don't always do the same with him. Ever since his unsuccessful attack, there are days when they don't consider the farm big enough for the three to them. To drive their point home the two geese have taken to ganging up on him. If they happen to come across him when he's taking a nap, they rush at him all fast and furious, wings spread out and flapping, tiny bead-like eyes shiny with malice. On these occasions TC does the only sensible thing: he dashes to the front door, where he sits ready to shoot indoors should they show signs of regrouping for a second attack. When it comes to overwhelming odds, this puss is no hero. A lion with the growl of a kitten, you say, but holy whiskers, those birds are a trial to him!

August, September, October. Summer turns to autumn, the days grow shorter, blue skies are more often grey, sun is replaced by rain. It's all very confusing. TC for one doesn't know which side of the door he wants to be on. When he's out he wants to come in and when he's in he immediately wants to be let out again. If it happens to be pouring outside, he curls up on Sophie's pillow and just lies there, peering over the edge through half-closed eyes. Should the rain last for more than a day or so, he gets dangerously restless – berserk, loopy, off the rails. You can find him up curtains, in and out of drawers, in closets. The house suddenly becomes too small to hold him and before long things begin to fly! Flower pots, ornaments and other fragile objects hit the floor. As a rule he's let off with a severe warning to behave himself, but the day he knocks down the Venetian vase he is banished to Millie and Frieda's shed for the rest of the day. In the evening, when Sophie goes to bring him in, he glares at her and burrows deeper into the hay.

'Come,' Sophie says, 'come in the warm. Really, you shouldn't be sulking. Mum was very fond of that vase. She brought it all the way back from Venice. It was very special to her.' TC doesn't stir, so Sophie pretends to leave. She can feel him watching her but resists turning round to see whether he's following. She's about to step outside when he rushes past her. Closing the door on Millie and Frieda and the three barncats, the two of them walk back to the cottage together.

When Sophie goes to say good-night to her parents, TC follows her. Sliding up to Mrs Miller, he rubs his back against her legs and begins to purr. 'Very nice,' Sophie's mother says, 'but what's it all in aid of?'

'I think he's trying to tell you he's sorry he broke your vase,' Sophie says, hurriedly appointing herself TC's interpreter.

'I see. Well, apology accepted,' Mrs Miller replies graciously.

Sophie picks up her cat and carries him to her room. 'You've done it again,' she tells him. 'Beats me how you always manage to get round them. Now, if I had broken that vase, I'd be sent to Coventry for a week.'

The black cat rubs his head against the side of her face, miaowing softly. 'Nothing to it, nothing to it,' he seems to be saying, 'With a little help from your friends, of course!'

As TC grows into a cat the wide-eyed kitten look is replaced by one of good-natured superiority. There are other changes too. He sleeps less, preferring to roam the fields for this and that – a field mouse here, a vole there, the odd snake and, to Sophie's regret, plenty of birds. But feasting on the creatures of the fields doesn't mean he wants less food at home. He eats and eats and eats, yet he doesn't get fat or sluggish and leaps about with effortless grace. And just as effortlessly he manipulates the humans around him to do his bidding: scratch him under the chin, knead the space behind his ears, stroke his belly, brush his coat. All he has to do is turn those amazing, green, lantern-like eyes on them. It works every time! He is spoiled rotten, just as Kid once told Sophie he would be. Yet everyone loves him. They just can't imagine life without him. Sprats, herrings, a piece of plump chicken, a bowlful of raw mince, a slice of juicy liver. They shouldn't but he's hard to deny. No wonder he baulks at his Kitty-Bites! He's had a taste of the good life.

And this desire for the very best does turn TC into a thief, just as Kid predicted back in the summer. It begins with what looks like a sudden loss of appetite. Sophie, worried about her pet, takes it up with her mother. 'You say he hasn't touched his food for days?' Mrs Miller asks.

'Doesn't go near it,' Sophie says, pointing to TC's bowl, still piled high with yesterday's dinner.

'Can't say I think he looks any thinner for it,' her father says, giving the hardened, dry mess a perplexed look.

'I bet he's all skin and bone under the fur,' Sophie shoots back.

'Hardly!'

'You don't think he might be ill?' Mrs Miller asks.

Mr Miller merely snorts at the suggestion. 'That cat has never looked healthier. He's eating all right, but where?'

Suddenly Sophie remembers the bet she and Kid made back in the summer. Might Kid be about to collect?

14

It's Sunday. Sophie, whose turn it is to clear away the breakfast things, has put everything in the sink and is about to go and look for her cat when he comes in lugging a piece of meat still wrapped in cellophane. Going right up to her, he drops it at her feet, as he does with all his 'catches'. Sophie's had presents from her pet before but never anything like this. As far as she can tell it looks very much like a leg of lamb. Sophie, too stunned to speak, looks from the meat to TC and back again. No doubt about it: this latest 'gift' is indeed a leg of lamb. She is about to take him to task over it when he walks out again. He is soon back though, this time trailing a string of chipolata sausages. Clearly pleased with the results of the day's 'hunt', he waits for the shower of praise which he considers he's more than earned. Sophie, shocked by the terrible discovery that her cherished pet has turned thief, thinks otherwise. 'Bad cat,' she scolds him, 'wicked cat, vile, thieving puss. Where did you lift all this?'

TC blinks. It's not what he expected. Humans! you never know where you are with them. Tail pointing stiffly up, he takes himself off. Pausing briefly in the

doorway to give her a long, reproach-laden look, he goes towards her room, the string of chipolatas still trailing behind him.

'Oh, no you don't,' Sophie shrieks, and hurls herself after him, outraged at the very cheek of it. 'You bring those bangers back here.'

She might as well save her breath. TC is dead set on having things his way over the sausages. Uttering a series of deep growls, he leaps into the wardrobe with his 'prey'.

Sophie's wondering how to get the chipolatas off him when she remembers the piece of meat still on the kitchen floor. What if her parents come in and find it. 'I'll deal with you later,' she calls out to the black cat, slamming the wardrobe door on him. Now for the leg of lamb. She can't go around asking who's lost a leg of lamb without also saying how it came to be in the house. Yet it seems a pity just to throw it away. Unless . . . She scoops up the meat, pushes it under her jumper and streaks out of the cottage, down the drive, out of the gate and on to Kid's house. At the gate there's Smith, just as she hoped he would be. He immediately begins to wag his tail at her, while uttering little yelps of welcome. Sophie looks around and puts her finger to her lips. 'Shhh . . .' she whispers, then pulls the leg of lamb out from under her jumper and throws it to him. 'Happy unbirthday, Smith,' she giggles and, turning on her heels, charges back the way she's come.

All out of breath, she flings herself on her bed, praying no one will come in until she is herself again. Especially not her Mum and Dad. Should they walk in on her now, she'll be hard-pressed for an explanation. But they don't, and when her heart has stopped pounding and is beating normally again she has this to say about her delinquent pet:

I have a little cat,
A stiff-necked puss,
Foot-loose, fancy-free
Go-as-you please –
His favourite game:
Stalking prey in cellophane.
And though strictly forbidden,
Raids next door's kitchen for his dinner.

Back home with his boodle,
He shuns interrogation.
Volunteers no explanation –
Coolly demands a standing ovation.
I think I'll tie his tail in knots
And put him on probation.

15

The next day on the way to school Kid tells Sophie how he found Smith tucking into a leg of lamb the day before. He tried to take it away but Smith acted so fierce he thought the dog might go for him if he pushed it, so in the end he left him to it.

'You tell your parents?' Sophie asks lightly.

Kid stares at her as if she's gone soft in the head. 'You crazy! Can you just imagine what would happen to Smith if I had!'

'What?'

'He'd be chained up now, that's what. I mean, that joint wasn't ours, so he must have nicked it from somewhere, right? Well, can you imagine the tongue-wagging there would be if folks found out the copper's tyke goes around snitching their Sunday dinners?'

'So what did you do?' Sophie says, carefully closing an eye at Smith.

'Nothing. Tore a strip off Smith and told him if he ever did it again I'd chain him up myself.'

'Fine,' Sophie says, 'except Smith isn't the thief.'

'What do you mean he's not the thief? I saw him with it, didn't I?'

'You saw him with it,' Sophie explains patiently, 'but he didn't steal it. TC did.'

'Go on,' Kid exclaims, eyes big as saucers.

'It's true. Cross my heart,' Sophie swears, and she goes on to tell him the whole sorry tale.

'Sophie Miller, I warned you this might happen, didn't I?' Kid says sternly. 'It's what comes of being too soft with animals, and talking of animals, you realize the trouble you might have landed Smith in had my folks stumbled on him with that meat instead of me. You acted real dumb, if I may say so.'

Sophie looks down at her feet. She can see Kid's point, but giving the meat to Smith had seemed the ideal, the only, solution at the time. 'Sorry, Kid,' she mumbles. 'I guess I didn't think. You know I'd never do anything to hurt Smith.'

'Yeah, I know,' he says in a calmer voice. 'Sorry I yelled at you, but you know how I feel about Smith. I'd die if anything happened to him.'

Sophie digs into the pocket of her school coat and brings up fifty pence, the cost of one copy of *Soccer Heroes*. 'Here,' she tells Kid. 'You won.'

'What's this for?' asks Kid. He's forgotten all about the bet.

Sophie reminds him. He says he doesn't want the money, but Sophie says he must take it. A bet is a bet. Kid gives in. He drops the coin into his pocket. 'You better make sure he doesn't do it again', he says, 'or folks are bound to put their heads together and, sooner or later, they'll get to the thief.'

'I know,' Sophie sighs. 'But how can I stop him? It will mean keeping an eye on him all the time.'

'Then that's what you'll have to do.'

'Suppose so.'

'Still,' Kid muses, his voice beginning to quiver, 'it is rather funny when you think about it. I mean, who would have thought it? A moggy hauling a leg of lamb all over the countryside. It's a RIOT.'

They look at one another and burst into laughter.

'Wonder what's for dinner today,' Kid yells.

'Laa–aa–mbert,' Sophie shrieks. Catching her right foot in her left hand she hops into the playground, yelling: 'Lamb, ram, roast ham.'

16

So, what's to be done? How is Sophie going to stop her feline felon from turning into a habitual criminal? Another sneak job like the last one and questions will be asked. Little notice is taken of small misdemeanours but, when they build up, they strike the eye. Next thing people will be out on their porches, firing at anything that moves. After giving the matter a great deal of thought, Sophie decides to invent a scapegoat. A fox! She'll put it about that a marauding fox is hijacking people's Sunday dinners right under their noses.

Mr and Mrs Miller have two sets of neighbours. Mr and Mrs White to the left and Mr and Mrs Macmillan to the right. Sophie decided to begin with Mrs Macmillan. Making out she's just passing, she strolls to the back of the Macmillans' cottage. Mrs Macmillan is busy hanging up her washing when Sophie arrives. After the usual pleasantries have been exchanged, Sophie tells Mrs Macmillan a fox has been seen going into people's kitchens, stealing their meat.

'Well,' says Mrs Macmillan cheerfully, her mouth full of pegs, 'he'll get no joy here. Mr Macmillan and I are vegetarians.'

'That's all right, then,' Sophie says, relieved. Making an innocent fox the scapegoat for her own pet's crimes lies heavily enough on her conscience as it is.

Her next visit is to Mr and Mrs White. Mrs White is out but Mr White is in the front garden, a cold pipe stuck between his teeth, about to set fire to a huge mound of leaves. 'Uncle Morris,' she calls out. She's known him all her life, so he's always been 'Uncle' Morris to her.

'Hello, Sophie,' he says. 'What can I do for you?' He walks over from his pile of leaves and comes to stand by the gate. While he waits to hear what is on her mind he takes the pipe out of his mouth and empties it by knocking it against the sole of his boot. He takes his tobacco pouch from his pocket and starts to fill his pipe. When he's finished, he returns the pouch to his pocket, strikes a match, puts it to the tobacco and begins to draw heavily. It's uphill work. As he battles to get the pipe going, Sophie pulls the one about the audacious fox. By the time she's finished, Uncle Morris has at last managed to light his pipe and is puffing away contentedly. 'A fox, you say,' he remarks thoughtfully. 'Why, now you mention it we did indeed lose a leg of lamb the other day. And a string of chipolatas. Insult on injury I call it.' He peers closely at her. 'A fox, eh?'

Sophie nods weakly. 'Uncle Morris,' she says, 'you . . . you wouldn't kill a ca– the fox I mean, if . . . if you came across it?'

'Noooo,' Uncle Morris says, pulling at the word as if it's an elastic band, 'but I'll sure pepper its backside for it, that I will. Got to teach old slyboots a lesson. Don't you agree?'

Sophie swallows hard. She's landed poor Rufus in it now! 'He . . . he won't come back,' she says hurriedly.

'How's that?'

'I . . . it wouldn't come back to the same place twice, would it?'

'And why not? Bet you my pipe last week's successful raid only served to whet his appetite for more of the same,' Uncle Morris says grimly.

Sophie can't see anyone wanting his old pipe – even if he, Uncle Morris, turns out to be right about the 'fox' returning to his kitchen a second time. 'Well, I'd better go,' she tells him. 'Goodbye, Uncle Morris.'

'Ay, and I best get back to my leaves. Well, thanks for warning me about the fox, young Sophie.' He starts to walk away, then turns his head and calls over his shoulder: 'A fox, eh? Maybe I'll give the pub a miss tonight.'

Sophie doesn't reply. She hopes the poor 'fox' won't get into trouble on account of her. She's quite forgotten the animal she's been discussing is an imaginary one. Talking about it has made it seem real.

Back home Sophie calls TC to her. A muffled miaow is heard from the wardrobe in her room; strangely enough, since she locked him in there it has become his favourite hiding-place. After a lot of coaxing, he comes out. Sophie picks him up and puts him on her lap. He immediately begins to purr and offers his neck for her to scratch. She will oblige, but first she's got something to tell him. 'Look here, mister,' she says sternly, 'you behave yourself. No more thieving or you'll land yourself in pots of trouble. From now on you take your meals in this house or you're likely to end up with a rump full of lead.'

The black cat gives her a lazy look out of his green, green eyes, yawns, stretches, tucks his paws under him and nods off.

'What will I do with you?' Sophie sighs.

She begins to stroke him; her mind is fixed on the unknown fox she's as good as delivered into Uncle Morris's hands. It makes her feel a real traitor.

17

As it happens a real live fox is caught, but not by Uncle Morris. It is December. Sophie, Kid and the rest of the gang are returning home from Saturday morning cinema in Lower Catsfield. On rounding one of the many bends in the lane, they as good as crash into none other than the terrible ogre, Farmer Stone himself, together with his dog The Beast and the fox, or at least a fox. The gun and the fox are both slung across Farmer Stone's back, the gun over his right shoulder, the fox over his left, its beautiful rust-coloured tail swinging like a pendulum to the movement of his body. It's alive but one of its legs is badly torn and bleeding.

The children jump back, eyes riveted on the gun and the wounded fox. Without warning Stone swings round. Eight little bodies turn to eight pillars of salt. The Ogre's grisly face, with its squashed nose, cavernous mouth, mean and moody eyes, wild salt-and-pepper eyebrows and skin the texture of cold porridge, is what bad dreams are made of. A deep silence steals over the lane. Even the birds stop in mid-song. It is so quiet the children fancy they can make out the sound of leaves falling.

The monster's lips move. For a moment it looks as if he is going to speak, but nothing comes of it. In the end he does not utter a sound, not a single word, and just turns and ambles on up the lane.

For a long time afterwards no one speaks. Only when the Ogre is no more than a speck on the horizon does the spell break. First to come out of it is Archie.

'Whoa! That poor Rufus. Taking it home to skin, I bet.'

'Why should he want to do that?' Indy wonders.

'You joking? There's good money in fox fur and badgers', rabbits', cats' and all kinds of skins.'

'Stop it,' Sophie demands.

Kid's arm shoots out to land squarely to Archie's chin.

'What's that for?' he screeches, reeling back.

'Pigeon brain,' Kid hisses.

'I was only winding you up,' Archie protests.

'Your mum must have spent the time she was carrying you watching horror movies,' Kid jeers.

'And yours was looking up the back end of a cow, I bet!'

Indy cuts in to tell everyone her mum told her she had a craze for chestnuts when she, Indy, was inside her, waiting to be born, and that's why she is so dark.

'You're black cause your dad's black, stupid,' Archie smirks.

Indy, long used to Archie's ways, shrugs her shoulders. 'I know it's not true about the chestnuts, but I still like hearing it,' she says.

Kid puts an arm around her. 'Berk,' he tells Archie.

Archie lets it go. He's got only one chin.

While the war of words is raging Sophie is working on something which, should it happen to reach the Ogre's ears, will leave him in no doubt as to the opinion the youngsters of Upper Catsfield have of him. 'Hey, you buzzards, listen to this,' she calls out.

Big bad Stone,
Teeth like tombstones,
Eye like millstones,
Nose a squashed toad,
Mouth like a black hole,
Gives kids nightmares,
Makes them groan,
Toss and turn –
The Devil take old Stone!

'Yeah!' everyone shouts. Even Archie, though it hurts his jaw plenty.

18

Before splitting up for lunch they agree to meet again that very same afternoon at Sophie's to discuss Farmer Stone. Something has got to be done to stop him trampling everyone's fields and shooting animals any old way he pleases.

'You'd think the countryside around here was all his private patch,' Sprat says indignantly.

'Listen everyone,' says Indy quietly, 'the fox hitching a ride on Stone's back was alive. I mean apart from its leg, it looked just fine. I know Archie thinks he's caught it to skin it, but if that was true then that fox would have been dead.

As always Archie has a ready answer. 'I told you, he's going to skin it only he must do it while its still alive or the pelt will lose in value.' He stresses 'alive' for extra effect.

Right then Sophie wishes him on another planet. 'Oh, go grab yourself a comet,' she tells him.

'Trouble with you creeps is you don't know a good yarn when you hear one.' Archie is sulking now.

Busker leans forward and snaps his fingers under Archie's nose.

'Archie Williams, you're pathetic.'

'You watch out I don't punch your face in,' Archie threatens.

Busker curls his hands into fists and begins to dance around him. 'Come on, funnyman. Hit us with a custard pie, then.'

'Shut your cakehole, cretin,' Archie throws at him, and then, to the others, 'See you later, creeps.'

'What's the rush?' The Squire wants to know.

Archie glances at his watch. '*The Phantom from Planet Zero*, that's what. On in seven mins.'

'Give it a miss, Arch. Let's ride over to the gravel pit on our bikes instead,' The Squire suggests.

Archie looks at him as if he's proposed something really weird and way-out. 'You kidding?' he cries, and then sets off at speed, his short, plump pins hardly touching the ground.

'He's a right case, that one,' is The Squire's honest opinion.

'Perhaps he'll grow out of it,' Indy says. 'Perhaps all he needs is a new interest or something.'

'If *The Phantom from Planet Zero* doesn't get him first,' The Squire mutters.

Titch begins to tug at Sprat's sleeve. 'Come on, Charlie. Mum will have our guts if we're late for lunch.'

Indy and The Squire too make ready to go. Kid is already walking away.

'Bye. Don't forget the meeting later on,' Sophie calls out and runs to catch up with Kid.

To begin with the meeting is mainly about tea and biscuits and fussing round TC. They all know the story of how the dying Snowflake carried him to Sophie's door in her mouth when he was still only a tiny kitten and this makes him kind of special. TC is a good sport. He lets himself be stroked, hugged, squeezed (rather too tightly for his liking at times) and cuddled. He chases catnip mice, bits of ribbon, marbles and pieces of string. He rolls on his back, pulls himself along the carpet on his paws, plays 'dead' – head thrown back, paws in the air – suffers his fur to be messed up – 'shaken and stirred' – Archie calls it, but enough is enough. There's only so much a cat can put up with without losing his dignity. Tail proudly erect, he retires from it all to lie on Sophie's pillow. Taking time to put his ruffled coat back in order, he then snuggles down in the feathers, tucks his paws under him, arranges his tail about him and sinks into sleep to the sound of ohs, ahs, and other cries of admiration from the children, all of it music to his ears.

The meeting can now begin in earnest. Someone suggests a petition, to be taken to Constable Brown, Kid's Dad. If enough people sign, he'll have to deal with Stone.

'When he gets the message folk round here don't care for him, maybe he'll hop it elsewhere,' says Sprat.

'Would be great not to have to bump into him ever again,' The Squire adds, remembering how they'd crashed into him in the lane.

'Yeah, but collecting names won't help any,' Kid informs them, 'because there's no law against scaring kids or carrying a gun, provided you have a licence for it. And the Ogre has.'

Sophie, who's been told as much by her own dad,

nods in support. 'It's what my dad says too,' she confirms.

Indy puts her hand up to speak. 'I know,' she says eagerly. 'Why don't we leg it over to Stone's and tell him how we feel about things ourselves?'

'Whaaat! You must be off your trolley,' the others shout in unison. The thought of coming face to face with the Ogre in his own lair doesn't bear thinking about.

'I'm not,' Indy protests. 'We could at least try it. The worst he can do is chase us away.'

'The worst he can do is to set The Beast on us, that's what,' Archie retorts grimly, and for once no one contradicts him.

Silence falls. Seems they've hit a brick wall. It is then that Sophie has her brainwave.

'Perhaps we shouldn't go there, but we could write to him,' she says tentatively.

The Squire's eyebrows shoot up into two perfect arches. 'You mean we should send a letter instead?'

'Exactly! That way no one gets hurt. We don't have to sign it or anything.'

However, Archie has a better idea – at least he thinks so. 'Let's send a couple of aliens to zap him.'

'And his dog,' Sprat slips in.

'Well, while you guys wait for them to land, the rest of us will take a vote on it,' Sophie tells them. 'Now then, who's for writing to Stone?'

All hands go up except Archie's. He looks about him. Appears he's the only one hanging back. In the end his hand goes up too – if only halfway.

'Right, that's everyone, then,' Sophie declares. She

takes paper and pencil and waits for someone to feed her the first line. No one does. It seems everyone present has forgotten how to talk. 'Come on, you muddlers. Use your loaves,' she goads them. 'What's come over you? No one's asking you to write a book. It's just a letter.'

'You write it and read it out to us,' Kid suggests shyly.

'All right.' Sophie chews the end of her pencil for a while before finally beginning to write. After a time she looks up from the paper in front of her. 'Ready?' They all nod. 'OK. Here goes:

Dear Farmer Stone

'How are you? We don't like the way you carry a gun about all the time. It looks scary and also it might go off by accident and hurt someone. And why must you kill so many animals? They don't bother you, so why can't you leave them alone?

That's all.'

Everyone thinks it's a good letter.

'Who is going to post it?' she asks.

'Why waste a stamp when we can take it to him?' Archie jeers.

'Yeah,' everyone shouts. 'Let Archie take it. He can take one of his aliens with him for protection.'

Archie is stumped. This is not what he meant. 'You gotta hope,' he mutters uncertainly, suddenly looking rather white about the gills.

'Archie's yellow,' Kid taunts him.

'You go, then, if you're so brave,' Archie spits back.

'Don't mind, as long as everyone else comes too.'

A lengthy discussion follows. For a while the camp is divided between those who think the letter should be posted and those keen for a spot of adventure to ginger things up a bit. Four in favour, four against. Archie, Titch, Sprat and The Squire against bearding the lion in his own den, with Sophie, Kid, Indy and Busker for it. A real tug-of-war! Looks like they might be at it all day. However, the problem is resolved by The Squire, who, offering no explanation for his change of allegiance, tips the scales by defecting to the opposite camp. Ignoring the insults hurled at him from his former 'allies', he suggests they ought to have a name for the venture. For his part, he thinks it should be called 'Operation Special Delivery'. Unless anyone has a better idea, of course. No one does. The codename is unanimously accepted. Now everything is set for the visit to Yew Tree Farm. The question is when?

'Let's go at night. It'll be more of an adventure that way,' Indy proposes.

The Squire agrees. 'Let's just hope he'll be asleep when we get there.'

'He might be roaming the fields,' Archie volunteers. 'My dad's seen him.'

'What's your dad doing out of bed nights?' the others want to know.

'Spotting UFOs, of course.'

'What! Here?' they chorus.

'Sure. One even landed in the field behind our house once.'

'Did you see it?' Busker sniggers.

Archie looks uncomfortable. 'Nooo . . .'

'Neither did anyone else,' Busker shouts, his face creased up with laughter.

19

Everyone is at the pond at the appointed hour. They talk in muted but light voices, the way you do when you are tense with excitement but don't want to make a show of it. All have been careful to come dressed in dark clothes. Archie has even taken the added precaution of blacking his face and the back of his hands with shoe polish. The others make fun of him and even Indy, normally so shy, ventures to crack a joke about it. 'No need to have gone to all that bother, Arch. All you have to do is walk behind me, man.'

It's a riot! The others quickly clamp their hands over their mouths to stop themselves from laughing out loud. Sound, as everyone knows, carries at night. Strangely enough Archie, a right hot-head usually and never lost for words, just shrugs his shoulders. Let them laugh . . .

The little band moves off. Keeping close together they creep stealthily up the high street, past the post office and newsagent's – run by Mrs Taylor, a lady with a keen eye, a sharp tongue and fussy ways; a right old trout in short – the greengrocer's – the proprietor there goes by the name of Amos Leek – the chemist's – proprietors Mrs and Mrs Purge – the butcher's – run by Mr Butley – the small supermarket – managed by the ever-smiling Mr Leach – the wool shop – belonging to the Misses Boone and their two Siamese cats, Sookie and Aki-San, who sleep wrapped around one another among the hanks of wool in the window – the off-licence – run by Mr Devlin and his handsome silver-grey tom Moonshine – and, a little further away, set back from the road and fronted by a large car park, the only pub for miles around, The White Cat, ruled by Mr King and the barmaid, Rita, all glitz and gossip. The children hurry past it, knees bent, heads low, arms pressed to their sides. It is after hours but one never knows . . . After the pub there's only one more house to consider: Old Jones's. The children tiptoe by – not that there's any need to, as everyone knows, the old codger is blind as well as deaf (as good as anyway) and generally hits the sack with the chickens. The youngsters don't know how old he is, but all agree he must have come out of the Ark.

So far so good, but once past Jones's house they are plunged into almost total darkness. No more street lamps, no friendly yellow lights to guide them and keep their spirits up. Switching on a torch is out of the question: the light could be spotted from the village, perhaps by Archie's dad, who might take it for a UFO!

'Ughh! Didn't think it'd be so dark,' Sprat murmurs.

'Scared of the dark, then?' The Squire says, all cocky, though really he feels far from confident.

'It's not the dark . . . it's what's in it,' Charlie mutters unhappily.

No one speaks. Sprat has hit the nail on the head! Waves of ice-cold sweat roll up and down their spines;

fear rides them as they tramp these dark, bleak fields where words die away and THINGS, whimsical and grotesque, come alive. Ghosts float in and out of the darkness, ghouls scream their silent screams, zombies, demons, vampires, werewolves – the stuff of which nightmares are made – come at them out of the inky, starless, moonless night. All human life seems to be elsewhere. Then, just when it feels as if all is lost, the blanket of cloud rolls back. A moon like a giant silver coin hangs in the sky and one by one the stars come out.

And with the light, courage returns. Once again they are cool cats of ACTION – bold, daring, cunning. Believe you can and you will! Fate loves the brave! Victory is only a matter of faith!

So, bright eyed and bushy-tailed once again, our fearless heroes march on the Ogre, eyes peeled for any sudden movements ahead, ears cocked for sounds spelling danger – a twig broken underfoot, the low, ferocious rumblings of monster or monsters about to attack, the 'click' of a trigger being pulled back. But – disappointingly – all is quiet. Not a squeak, not a whisper.

Stone's farm is as dark and silent as space itself. Sticking close together, they hot-foot it to the front door. The idea is to deliver the letter and beat it, but now that they are at their goal the fizz suddenly goes out of the night, cruelly deflating the fabulous sense of adventure of a while ago. The 'zip' and 'zap' must somehow be injected back into it or the whole thing will turn as cold and flat as yesterday's pancakes. And who better to start things rolling again than

Archie. Sensing he might never get another opportunity to look over an ogre's lair, he puts his hand on the doorhandle and turns it. The door swings open with a noise loud enough to wake the dead. Everyone freezes. If Stone is in there, he must have heard. But when several minutes pass and nothing at all happens, they grow bold again.

'Come,' Archie urges. 'Might as well take a peek at things now we're here.'

'Go in there? You must have a tile loose,' Kid whispers.

'It's all right. Stone and The Beast aren't here. You don't think we would have got this far if they were, do you?'

'Better cautious than reckless,' Kid mumbles, but he follows the others in.

Busker switches on his torch. Holding on to one another, they follow the slim beam of light down the narrow hall. Stone's home is a small two-up two-down, with bedrooms upstairs, kitchen and lounge downstairs. The first room they come to is the lounge. It's in no way unusual or markedly different from many others. A couch and two armchairs in front of the fireplace, a clock and some odds and ends on the mantlepiece, a sideboard, a couple of elegant-looking chairs that don't fit in but seem to have come from another kind of life entirely, and a carpet which, even in the dim light from Busker's torch, looks as though it's seen better days. That's all. No bones, no arms or legs, to indicate that the Ogre lives on a diet of little boys and girls – or their pets. In fact, the room is surprisingly clean and tidy. Not sure whether to feel relieved or just let down, they troop out again and go on to the next room, the kitchen. They find the door closed. Kid hesitates and then, with a look of resolution on his face, he grabs the handle, turns it and gives the door a push with his foot. It swings back, coming to a stop against the wall. Everyone surges forward to peer over his shoulder. He is about to ask Busker for the torch when . . .

'Eeeeeee!' A bloodcurdling cry from Titch sends everyone scuttling back down the hall, the hairs on their heads shocked to attention.

'What is it? What is it?' they all call out nervously.

'Don't know but it stared straight at me,' Titch sobs.

Busker pushes the torch into Archie's hand. 'You take a look. Whatever is in there won't see you.'

Archie can't figure out what Busker is talking about, but then he remembers his blackened face. Quick as a flash he passes the torch to Indy. For once he is content to take a back seat. 'Here, Indy, you have it,' he says. He knows he is showing a yellow streak as wide as a church door but right now FEAR rules.

Indy takes the torch. 'See, you're walking behind me after all,' she laughs. 'Now, you best stay close if you don't want the bugaboos to get you.'

Archie doesn't need to be told twice. Together they go off to investigate what it was that gave Titch such a fright. Coming to a halt by the kitchen door Indy sends the light from the torch dancing over the room and picks up first one pair of eyes, then another and another. The room, in spite of the silence, is alive.

'Animals. Lots of them. In cages,' they call out to the others. They are right. The kitchen is crammed full of them. Owls, rabbits, badgers, some large birds. (Sprat thinks they are crows, but it's difficult to make out), a kestrel, one wing taped to his body, and a fox. A fox?

'Look everyone,' Indy says, 'isn't this the fox we saw hitching a ride on Stone's back?'

They all peer closely at it. It certainly looks like the same one. At any rate, its front leg is all bandaged up.

'Think you're right,' says Archie. He points to the cages containing the furry animals. 'Told you! Five . . . six good pelts right here.'

Titch is puzzled. 'Why should he go to the trouble of bandaging them and things if he's going to skin them anyway? Doesn't make sense if you ask me.'

'He has to wait for the fur to grow back over the wound. Everyone knows you lose money if the pelt isn't perfect,' Archie informs him.

'And the owls? You can't skin them.'

'No, but they can be plucked, whacko,' Archie sneers.

'Why should he want to do that?'

'Probably sells the feathers for dusters and things.'

'Archie Williams,' Kid says, 'you sure are one for the broad-brush approach.'

'Well, it's plain to see what he's at,' Archie replies confidently. He takes the torch from Indy and shines it over the rest of the room. A dresser, a sideboard, a small grandfather clock, four chairs – one of which is occupied by three cats, who, having given the intruders a long, steady look, lose all interest in them and go back to sleep. Archie pretends to wipe his eyes. 'Poor puddies, the ogre'll soon have the coats off your backs.'

'You shut up, Archie Williams, or I'll . . .' Sophie begins. She doesn't finish the sentence. Instead she, like the others, follows the beam of light as it sweeps over the table, revealing traps, snares, knives, scalpels in all shapes and sizes, hypodermic syringes and sinister-looking bottles with skull and crossbones labels. They hold their breath. It's so quiet you could easily pick up the sound of a speck of dust hitting the floor.

'Now do you believe me?' Archie asks triumphantly. 'Or maybe you want to hang around till he gets back and ask him. "Please, Farmer Stone, do you torture animals, skin them, pluck them, do 'orrible things to them? We won't tell, cross our hearts."'

'Just because he has those things, doesn't mean he uses them to torture animals,' Indy tries tentatively.

Archie glares at her. 'No, then what are they for?'

It is all rather fantastic. The general opinion is that Archie must be right. What other explanation can there be for this collection of spine-chilling instruments? Temporarily lost for words, they look on the awesome tools of pain and misery, unable (perhaps even unwilling) to believe such a monster is living among them.

Sophie is first to speak. 'Look,' she says, 'there's only one thing for it. We've got to set these animals free. We'll carry the cages outside and open them and that will be that.'

Everyone's for it. Sophie is right. They can't go and leave the poor creatures behind now they know what's in store for them. 'At least they won't end up as purses and gloves and shaving brushes . . . and as snacks for The Beast.'

They are all set to start removing the cages from the kitchen to the yard when the silence is shattered by a series of rapid ominous-sounding barks, so loud they might be coming from right inside the house.

'Shakes, it's The Beast and he sounds like he's in the next room,' Sprat squeaks.

'Don't be daft. You really think he would have let us come this far if he was?' The Squire retorts with a confidence he doesn't really feel. Still, one has got to check the panic before it gives them all the horrors. It doesn't quite work.

'Stone's coming back. He and The Beast will be on us any minute,' Titch whimpers.

That's all it takes to start the others off. 'We'll end up skinned too . . .'

'Plucked . . .'

'Dissected . . .'

'Morsels for The Beast . . .'

The Squire, less confident now, decides the time is ripe for retreat. 'Let's rip, you bugbears,' he commands, doing his best to keep his voice from shaking.

The scramble for the door is immediate. 'Don't forget the letter, Soph,' Indy shouts. Sophie lets it drop as if it has suddenly become too hot to hold.

Once out, they streak across the yard and back

over the fence like bats out of hell, collecting lumps, bumps and bruises as they go. Next time they want to send a letter, they'll make sure they use Her Majesty's postal services!

20

How do things look?
Ugh!
That bad?
Worse!

From that time on Stone, the letter and, of course, the animals in his kitchen are always on the children's minds. Not a day passes without their wondering whether Stone saw them leaving his place and whether he found the letter. How they wish they had the time to set free those poor, helpless creatures now facing such a grim future. Oh, it's all so very desperate, such an unholy mess. If only they hadn't put themselves in such an impossible position, if only they could talk to somebody about that night. But, of course, they can't. Delivering a letter is one thing but breaking into someone's home is a different kettle of fish altogether. If only there was a way of alerting people to what was going on up at Stone's without giving themselves away. Or should they bite the bullet and spill the beans and blow the consequences? Tell the truth and shame the Devil and all that? Or again, might not the whole ghastly business go away if they simply pretend it never happened? They try the latter, but of course, it doesn't work. Some things just won't go away. What is done cannot be undone. Boy! Some Christmas this one promises to be!

The days drag by. Racked with remorse and fearful for their hides should the whole thing come out, they have a hard time of it. With Christmas only a week away, getting into the spirit of things is uphill work. They are too tired for one thing. None of them sleeps too well nowadays. As they get ready for bed each evening, they steel themselves for the nightmares they know lie in wait. Why, oh why hadn't they posted the wretched letter? None of this would have happened then!

In her bed, dozing fitfully, Sophie, worn to a frazzle by guilt-ridden days and restless nights, becomes aware of gentle tapping at the french windows. Rubbing her eyes, she staggers out of bed, wondering who is at her door at this hour. She puts on the light and flicks one of the curtains aside. To her surprise it's Kid. Kid and Smith. Wide awake now, she unlocks the door and lets them in. 'What's the matter? What are you two doing out in the middle of the night?' she whispers.

'I'm running away and I'm taking Smith with me,' Kid informs her.

'What, now?'

'No point in waiting. I've made up my mind to go and I'm going. Thought I'd come to say goodbye first, that's all.'

'Why does it have to be now?'

'Not going to stick around for someone to go soft and let the cat out of the bag about "Operation Special Delivery", am I? I'll split now before the muck hits the fan.'

Sophie does see his point. Things are pretty bleak (and might get bleaker still), but to leave home now, with Christmas just around the corner!

'I know what you are thinking,' Kid says, 'but I don't give a fig about Christmas. It's fine for you, but it's the usual slog for me. All I get is work, work, work. As soon as I'm through with one thing it's on to something else. Well, I've had it. Up to here!'

Listening to him, Sophie recalls once telling him that if he did ever run away she wanted to be in on it. Looks like the time has come to turn her words into action. 'Oh, well,' she says, stifling a yawn, 'seeing you really have made up your mind to go, I'll come with you. If you don't mind me tagging along, that is?'

Kid shakes his head. 'I don't, but there's no need for you to run away. All you'll get is a good dressing-down and that will be that.'

'Kid Brown, there are dressing-downs and dressing-downs,' Sophie points out.

Kid still doesn't look sure. 'It could be dangerous, you know.'

'I know, but we have got Smith. You said yourself he isn't afraid of anything.'

'He isn't.'

'Well, then, we've got nothing to worry about. Anyway, TC's coming too.'

He stares at her as if she's suddenly gone quite

mad. 'You are not thinking of taking a cat along, Sophie Miller.'

'I just said so, didn't I.'

'Well, as long as you don't expect me to help look for him if he runs away.'

'He won't. Anyway if he does, he'll come back here. Cats are wizards at finding their way home.'

Kid shrugs his shoulders. 'Well, it's your cat.'

'Right,' Sophie says. 'Now, just hang on while I scribble a note to my folks.'

'Really, Soph, you don't have to run away just because I am.'

'I know, but I want to. Are we best friends or aren't we?'

At this Kid gives in. Secretly he's glad. Sophie's a brick!

'By the way, have you brought any provisions?' Sophie asks Kid.

He looks blank.

'You know, FOOD.'

Kid shakes his head. Sophie is amazed that he should have overlooked something as important as food.

'I've been kind of mixed-up of late,' Kid offers by way of excuse.

'That's all right. You just wait here while I go to the kitchen,' Sophie tells him. Quiet as a mouse she tiptoes to the kitchen, followed by TC. She quickly helps herself to whatever is at hand, enough for herself, Kid and, of course their four-legged friends. Including some of the ham left over from supper, she looks down at her cat. What I do for you!' she whispers to him. He presses himself against her leg and draws a wet, rasping tongue over it. 'Much obliged, I'm sure,' he seems to be saying.

Gently closing the fridge door, they return to Sophie's room as silently as they left it. She packs her booty into a little rucksack, then sits down at her desk to write a note to her parents. It goes like this:

Dear Mum and Dad

If I don't show up for breakfast, DON'T WORRY.
If I'm not back for lunch, DON'T BE MAD.
If I'm not in for tea, DON'T FRET.
If I'm still not here for dinner, DON'T PANIC.
If I'm not in my bed tonight, DON'T CRY.

PS I have taken TWO rolls, TWO bars of chocolate, TWO apples, TWO bags of crisps, SOME ham.

I tell you this so you'll know I've not gone alone.
Sophie
xxx

21

The night is cold. Sophie and Kid walk close together, heads low, hands thrust deep in their pockets for extra warmth. Smith is keeping step with Kid while TC is riding piggyback on Sophie. He's made himself comfortable on top of her rucksack, his head pressed against her ear, tail dangling limply down her back.

On and on they go, doggedly crossing field after field, the frozen grass crunching under their feet like broken glass, the sharp, snow-scented air stinging their nostrils.

'Think it will snow?' Kid asks, little clouds of steam escaping from his mouth with every word to rise and float before him like tiny ghosts.

'Hope so. Would be nice with a white Christmas for a change, wouldn't it?' Sophie replies wistfully. 'We could go sliding down the lane and have snow-ball fights and . . .' She stops abruptly. She has just remembered they won't be anywhere near the lane then. All at once she feels out of sorts – grumpy, tired, fed up with the whole idea of running away. 'I wish we hadn't taken this roundabout way to the road,' she moans. 'We'd be half way to I'chester by now if we'd stuck to the lane as usual.'

'And risked being caught in the headlights of some car like a couple of hares,' Kid snaps.

It's true. The way over the fields affords them better protection, even though it does add a good mile or so to an already long road. The direction they are moving in will take them past old Jones's place but they don't foresee any trouble from that quarter. The old man is not likely to be roused from his slumbers by the two of them walking past his door. The only other farm vaguely on their route is Stone's and it's certainly not in their plan to look in on him this night!

Stone! The mere thought of him, and his murderous dog, brings a touch of evil to the silent, brooding landscape. Familiar, everyday objects suddenly take on the most fantastic shapes. Rocks become boulders about to be hurled at them by enemies existing only in their own imaginations. The lower branches of a tree turn into clawed hands to grab at them as they pass. Hedges that were just hedges moments ago are now sinister hiding-places affording cover to all kinds of horrors – none of them looming larger than Stone himself, crouching in the darkness, gun at the ready, dog at his side, ready to hurl itself at them and tear them to pieces on the order of its master.

It's all too much. Feeling their stomachs turn over in fear, they make a run for Jones's cottage and throw themselves on to a rickety, worm-eaten old wooden bench just inside the porch. With a loud groan, it gives way beneath them. Sprawled among the splintered remains, they blink and look about them. Talk of being knocked all of a heap! Forgetting where they are, they explode in riotous laughter. The animals, not wanting to be left out of the fun, join in, Smith jumping all over them, barking playfully, TC running in and out between everyone's legs, frisky as a kitten.

Sophie suddenly clamps her hand over her mouth to stop any further outbursts. 'Ssshhhh,' she hisses at the others, 'or you'll bring Jones down.'

Kid looks up, giving the dark windows a scathing look. 'Don't worry about him. The turnip-basher is as deaf as a doorpost.'

'You'd better be right,' Sophie mutters and, crawling out of the debris, goes to sit on Jones's front step. She opens the rucksack and begins to rummage about in it. Suddenly she's very hungry. 'What'll you have?' she asks Kid.

'What is there?'

'Rolls, apples, chocolate, crisps.'

'Crisps, I think.'

She pulls out two bags. 'Bacon or cheese and onion?'

'Bacon, please.'

He catches the bag she throws at him and comes to sit beside her. 'That bench is no good for anything but the fire, now, I'm afraid,' he says with a touch of regret.

But Sophie already has the answer to that little problem. 'Don't worry. I'm sure my mum will put together a new one for him if I ask her.'

'How will you ask her when you're not going to be here?' Kid says, reminding her they are leaving Catsfield, perhaps for ever.

Sophie looks pensively into the night. 'Let's not talk about it,' she says quietly, and changes the subject by

telling Kid he ought to have put on an extra woolly under his jacket and a pair of decent shoes. 'You don't wear plimsoles to run away in. At least not in winter,' she scolds him.

'Guess you're right,' he agrees, 'but it's too late to do anything about it now. Any case, my feet are already like clumps of ice.'

'So will the rest of you be soon, the way you're dressed.'

'So what? I don't care, do I?'

'Think of your mum and dad. It'd ruin their lives if you were to be brought home all stiff, like a piece of frozen fish.'

'Serve them right, I say.'

'Kid Brown,' Sophie says primly, 'that's no way to speak of your mum and dad.'

'What a little Miss Proper we've suddenly turned into,' he sneers.

'Well, you shouldn't. I'm sure they'd be worn to shadows with crying if anything really bad happened to you.'

'Fat lot they'd care. They might be put out at finding themselves short of a pair of hands, but that's all. If I know them they'll soon be telling everyone – the butcher, the baker, the candlestick maker – how lazy I always was and that I never showed much sense,' Kid spits out bitterly.

'That's not true. You are not lazy and you have oodles of sense,' Sophie cries loyally.

'Thanks. Nice to know someone thinks so.' Kid stands up. 'Best get a move on or we'll both of us end up stiff as logs.'

Sophie, her backpack once more in place, gets up too, but slowly.

'What is it?' Kid asks, a little anxiously, thinking maybe she has changed her mind and is about to turn back.

'Nothing . . .'

'Come on. You don't fool me. You've had some kind of brainwave, right?'

'Hm . . .'

'Come on!'

'Well . . .'

'Quit stalling, Sophie Miller, or I'll make off without you,' Kid says angrily.

'Don't rush me, Kid Brown, or it might be me who goes without you,' she hits back.

'OK. I'm going to count to ten. If you haven't stopped chewing the cud by then, we split company, right?'

'Boy, you are one for flying off the handle, aren't you?' Sophie teases him.

'I hate half-finished sentences, that's why. Hedging is naff, real girl stuff,' Kid sneers.

'I was just thinking,' Sophie says slowly, ignoring his remarks about girls, 'that we might go by Yew Tree Farm.'

Kid is aghast. 'What for?'

'A spot of unfinished business, perhaps?'

A deep furrow appears between Kid's eyes. Then the penny drops. 'You want another go at freeing those animals,' he exclaims.

Sophie nods, but Kid shakes his head. 'What if he's still up?'

'He won't be. Probably he's out. Like last time,' she says confidently, forgetting that only a short while back the thought of Stone tramping the fields had had them running like hares.

Still Kid hesitates. 'If we're caught . . .' he begins, letting the rest of the sentence hang in the air.

'We won't be.'

Kid digs his toe into a clod of earth, breaks it up, swings his leg back and with a mighty kick sends the bits flying into the darkness. 'OK, then,' he agrees. He is still not sure they are doing the right thing, but the chance of succeeding draws him to Yew Tree like a magnet.

'Good old Kid. I knew I could count on you!' Sophie cries.

'Good old Kid,' Kid mimics, then adds glumly, 'Bet I'll regret it.'

'Just keep in mind how good it will feel to know the poor little beasts are out of his clutches,' Sophie comforts him.

'Yeah. Anyway, let's get a move on. It'll be light soon and we aren't anywhere near the road yet.'

They are about to move off when a voice, sounding like one of those old records full of cracks and crackles that Sophie's Grandad Ned thinks so much of, roots them to the spot. Old Jones, wrapped in a threadbare tweed coat reeking of mothballs, with a hat that must have been the hottest in hat-fashions way back in the dark ages, appears at the door and demands he be allowed to go along with them. Sophie glares at Kid. 'Deaf as a doorpost, is it?'

'We . . . we aren't going anywhere, Mr Jones,' Kid tries.

'Save your breath to cool your porridge, young fellow. I heard you. You are going to Stone's, and seeing he's the one that did my Jack in, it's only right I should give him a piece of my mind.'

'It's a long way, Mr Jones,' Kid tries again.

'Don't you worry about me,' Jones says, waving him aside. 'I'll have you know I'm one of the great walkers around here.'

'Was, I think,' Sophie mutters under her breath.

'OK, then,' Kid tells the old man, 'but if anything goes wrong, you're on your own. On this expedition it's everyone for themselves.'

'Yes, yes. Now let's hit the trail, you impudent rascals. I'm dying to see that rogue's face when I give him what for.'

The two steal glances at one another. Dying's right!

'I expect you'll scare him out of his wits, Farmer Jones,' Sophie mutters sarcastically.

'I have clashed with many a bully in my time, young miss, and I swear to you no one's ever got the better of me. No, sir,' the old man boasts in his cracked voice. The declaration cuts no ice with Kid.

'Sure, way back when Adam was a nipper,' he says between his teeth.

Of course, there is no way the old boy, frail as a whisper, wizened as a prune, pigeon-toed and pigeon-chested, can keep up with them. All too soon he is lagging behind. The youngsters stop to wait for him. Wheezing, shuffling, snuffling and, as often as not, stumbling over his own feet, he cuts a sorry figure. Feeling sorry for him, the children take hold of an arm each and walk him between them. He is so light they could easily lift him clear off the ground if they wanted to – but they don't. In spite of all those cutting remarks earlier, they are not out to make fun of him.

After an age, they at last see Yew Tree Farm. Letting go of Jones, they all three enter the Ogre's camp stealthily. As they near the front of the cottage they see a light in one of the downstairs windows. It must be coming from the kitchen. Of course! What better time for an Ogre to be torturing his poor, helpless victims than the deep of night? Smith, drawing close to Kid, sniffs the air and begins to whine softly. The smell and the feel of danger are everywhere.

TC, who has been amusing himself jumping in the ice-filled furrows ever since the party left Jones's place, begins to weave in and out of Sophie's legs, asking to be put back on her shoulder. She scoops him up and drapes him across her neck, and there he stays, head up, emerald eyes piercing the night like two livid flames of green fire, ears cocked towards the lighted window, whiskers twitching, tail lashing furiously.

They wait, but the minutes pass without anything happening. Sophie's arm shoots out in a wide gesture which takes in the whole farm. 'Doesn't look as if anyone is here after all.'

Kid is not convinced. 'What about the light, then?'

Sophie laughs it off. 'Relax, will you. Perhaps he's only left it on to keep burglars away. Lots of people do.'

A look of surprise crosses Kid's face. 'We don't.'

'No need to with a copper in the house, is there?' she snickers.

'Oh, yeah. I forgot,' says Kid.

Old Jones, growing impatient, totters off in the direction of the light. Sophie and Kid follow. On reaching the house, they press themselves against the wall on either side of the window, taking care not to stray into the patch of light. Not so Jones, though. Before they know what is happening he hurls himself at the window and begins to beat the grimy panes, now with his knuckles, now with the flat of his hand, setting the whole thing a-rattling in its frame.

'You old rascal, you scoundrel, where's my Jack? I want my dog, you hooligan,' he shouts at the top of his cracked, croaky voice.

Trembling like leaves in a storm, Kid and Sophie look to see who it is Jones is showering with abuse. It is Stone, sitting at a table with an owl lying lifeless before him. In his hand is a small, sharp knife which he looks to be about to plunge into the bird. Or would, had he not been staring at the wild, gesticulating figure of Jones, eyes on stalks, mouth hanging open like a black hole.

'What now?' Sophie moans.

'Put your feet on the starting-block,' Kid tells her. 'Run, Sophie, run!'

And that's just what they do. Once again they are fleeing Stone's place. Not until they have put a whole field and a half between them and Yew Tree Farm do they dare stop and look back. 'Holy Wurzel, we've left Old Jones behind,' they call out together, taking the words out of each other's mouths.

'The old scarecrow has only himself to blame. If he hadn't let off like that . . .' Sophie begins.

'I feel awful about it.'

'Me too.'

'So much for Stone not being at home,' Kid mocks.

Sophie twists her face into a grimace. 'So I was wrong. Question is, what do we do now?'

'Go home,' says Kid.

'What!'

'We go home,' Kid repeats.

'And leave Jones to Stone?'

'Well, no . . .' Kid replies, though he doesn't suggest they go back for him either. But he does point out to Sophie that TC is no longer on her shoulder.

'Must have jumped off when we started running, but it's all right. He'll make his way home when he's had his fill of being out. He often stays away all night,' Sophie answers. She's not worried. TC has always come home before. Right now it's not her cat she's worried about but Old Jones. 'What are we going to do about him?' she asks Kid.

'Nothing,' Kid says flatly. 'Jones is so old and wizened, even if The Beast does get him, he's sure to spit him out again.'

Sophie shakes her head. 'Kid Brown, there are times when you sound just like Archie Williams.'

'Don't you get all prickly with me,' Kid bites back. 'Going to Stone's was your idea.'

'You didn't have to come if you didn't want to.'

'Didn't have much choice, did I?'

'I didn't exactly have to twist your arm.'

'Oh, let up, will you? Well, I'm off home. You coming or not?'

'Thought we were running away?' Sophie says cuttingly.

Kid makes a face. 'It can wait. Perhaps I'll settle for telling my folks a thing or two instead. Time I made it clear I won't take being kicked around any more.'

Sophie decides to overlook the exchange they've just had. 'That's right,' she shouts heartily, 'that's it, old mate. Stand up and be counted, that's what I say.'

'Steady on. Haven't done it yet.'

'But you will. I know you will.'

Kid grins. 'Who knows, maybe I'll turn chicken when it comes to it.'

'No, you won't!'

'Thanks, pal.'

'How about tonight's little disaster? Do we tell any one?'

'We'll just sit tight and see which way the cat jumps, all right?'

'Fine by me.'

'Bound to catch up with us in the end, I guess,' Kid muses.

Sophie nods. It makes her go all weak inside when she thinks just how deep in trouble they are but all the same, she is glad to be going home. To her mum and dad, Christmas and, of course, her cat.

22

But when Sophie does creep back to her room after leaving Kid, TC is not there. Looks like he decided to make a night of it, whatever he's doing out there. Scanning the room for him, her eye falls on the note she left for her parents earlier on. Before getting into bed she puts it in the drawer of her desk. What they don't know won't pain them. They'll ask no questions and she won't have to tell any lies. And now, at last, to bed. She beats her pillow into shape, puts her head down on it and soon she's fast asleep, the events of the night banished to the very back of her mind.

Sophie doesn't wake up till well into the morning the next day. As soon as she opens her eyes, she looks for her cat, expecting to find him curled up next to her all warm and soft, his tail hanging over the edge of the bed, his face buried in her hair. Instead, his place beside her is empty and cold. She tears off her nightie, pulls on a pair of jeans and a sweater and makes straight for the kitchen. On the way she throws a quick look around her parents' bedroom, the bathroom, the airing-cupboard (he often likes to curl up in there, especially on really cold nights and last night was very cold), the lounge and, lastly, the kitchen. There is no sign of the black cat anywhere. Sophie opens the door and begins to call for him, softly at first and then louder and louder.

Shivering, she waits in the doorway, hoping for a sign of him, but though she stands there till she's frozen through, the black cat does not show himself. Throwing a jacket over her shoulders and slipping her feet into boots, she walks round to the front of the house. A thin layer of snow, clean and crisp, covers the ground. She lifts her eyes up to the leaden sky. More on the way too. Maybe she and Kid will get the white Christmas they wished for last night.

The car is not in the drive. Sophie is disappointed her mum and dad have driven off without her. She is sure they've gone shopping in I'chester, and she did so want to go with them. She loves the noise and bustle of shopping for Christmas. On the other hand, it does mean she can go on looking for her cat and get her chores over with before they return. Going back, into the house, she takes the pail and goes to milk Millie and Frieda. Maybe she'll find TC there? Could be he is curled up in the hay with his three 'uncles', Benny, Max and Yoghurt, snug as a bug and just not wanting to get his nose cold. But, once again she is disappointed. The goats are alone in their shed.

Sitting on her little milk stool beside them she wonders with sudden alarm whether history is about to repeat itself. She finishes the milking and before leaving the shed she fills a dish to the brim with fresh milk for the cat. 'TC, TC,' she calls softly. 'But it's no use. No black cat comes bounding out of the shadows, no green eyes meet hers. TC is gone. Vanished. On her way out, Sophie stops to rub the knobbly heads of the goats. The idea of history repeating itself begins to haunt her. First Snowflake and now TC. No, it can't be, it mustn't be . . .

Crushed, she returns to the house to wait for her parents. On hearing the car, she rushes out and begins to fire questions at them before they've even had time to get out. 'Mum, Dad, have you seen TC this morning? Did he come to have his breakfast? Did . . .'

'Steady on,' her father says, 'and it's "No" on both counts. Now, how about lending a hand with this?' He throws open the boot.

Sophie's eyes grow round in her face and for a moment she forgets about her cat.

'You've really burnt money this time,' she says, impressed.

'Just the same as any other Christmas,' her mother laughs, then, 'Wait till you see what we got for TC.'

Sophie almost spills the beans about last night then. It's only the thought of what Mr Brown might have in store for Kid that stops her. Instead she swallows hard and says: 'He's not here, Mum.'

'He'll come,' her mother replies. 'Have you ever known him to miss lunch?'

Sadly there's a first time for everything. TC does miss lunch. And not only that day but the next, and the one after that too. At night Sophie, wrapped in a blanket, her pillow under her arm, goes to sleep by the french windows with the curtains drawn right back and the light on. The light is for TC, to guide him home, let him know she hasn't given up on him.

Every night fresh snow falls. It piles up in enormous drifts against houses, walls, on hedges and the branches of trees, where it sits like dollops of whipped cream. No one can remember it ever having snowed like this. It's a record! No doubt about it! They are in for the sparkliest, whitest Christmas ever. No need for 'canned' snow this year!

Christmas Day arrives but to one little girl it means nothing. Christmas morning doesn't put a sparkle in *her* eyes. Huddled inside her dressing-gown, her face whiter than the snow outside, dark circles round her eyes, she wanders through the cottage like a small, forlorn ghost. 'I should have worried about TC instead of silly Old Jones,' she mutters to herself, blind to the cheerfully decorated rooms, the Christmas tree with its baubles and tinsel, the pile of parcels under it, the kitchen smelling of herbs and spices. At this point she begins to cry. She's cried so often these last days it's a wonder she has any tears left.

And, as if she hasn't enough on her mind already her mother hands her a letter she says must have been delivered by hand, as of course there is no post on Christmas Day. It is addressed to Miss Sophie Miller, Baytree Cottage, Upper Catsfield, in large, ornate, kind of old-fashioned letters, but that's all. No stamp, no name on the back to indicate who the sender is. Sophie shrugs and tears open the envelope. Inside is a Christmas card, a pretty card with lots of snow and robins and holly, and a sweet little ditty, but no name. Whoever put it through the letter box has forgotten to sign it.

'Who is it from, pet?' Mrs Miller asks, her curiosity getting the better of her.

Sophie passes the card to her. 'Don't know. It's not signed,' she replies dully.

'Someone must have got Christmas mixed up with Valentine's Day,' her mother jokes.

Sophie doesn't hear, doesn't care. She will never care about anything again. No, it's not true. She does care. Not a moment goes by when her mind isn't on a black, black, black cat with cool-green eyes, ice-cream-pink tongue and charcoal-grey whiskers.

23

On Boxing Day the gang, led by Kid, call on Sophie. They are going to go sledging down the lane. Unsalted and unsanded, it makes a great run. 'Come on,' they shout, waving trays, plastic bags and sheets of corrugated plastic at her, the nearest they have to sledges – except The Squire, who has a real one, made of wood with brass runners.

Sophie doesn't want to go, but they say they'll stage a sit-in outside her door till she does. Very reluctantly, she follows them into the bright freezing sunlight.

For that morning at least Sophie is herself again. She actually manages to put aside her sorrow and enjoy things. It's a long time since she's had any fun. Riding behind Kid on his piece of plastic sheeting, her arms thrown round his waist, her hair flying behind her as they hurtle down the lane, smooth as polished glass, face aglow, eyes sparkling.

Taking a break to get their breath back, Kid asks her if she's let on about Old Jones yet at home. Sophie says no, she hasn't been able to think of anything but her cat. 'I went over to his place to check if he's come back. I knocked and knocked on his door for ages. If he was in there, he would have heard me,' Kid says.

'You don't think he's as deaf as a doorpost anymore, then?' Sophie teases him.

'You are not going to throw that at me again, are you?'

Sophie shakes her head. 'I was only needling you. Anyway, I wouldn't worry about him. He's bound to turn up sooner or later.'

But Kid is not an easy one to convince. 'We shouldn't have left him, Soph. What if he has been murdered, or is lying frozen in a ditch?'

'Has it been noticed he's not been around lately?'

'Don't think so. Everyone was too busy before Christmas and I heard Mum tell Dad his daughter must have come and taken him to London with her for the holidays.'

Suddenly a new thought strikes Kid. 'Say, you don't think Old Jones and the Ogre hit it off and decided to spend Christmas together and are having the time of their lives while we sit here worrying ourselves sick over the old scarecrow?'

'Well, if he is, I hope Stone's cooking gives him a right old bellyache.'

'All the same, if he's not back by the end of the week, I'm telling my dad. OK?'

Sophie makes a wry face. 'If you like.'

And now they've reached a decision about Jones, Sophie goes back to mourning her missing cat. 'I've got to find TC, I've got to,' she tells Kid.

'If we only knew here to look.'

'He's got be around here somewhere.'

'Wouldn't he have shown up by now if he was?'

Sophie's lips begin to tremble. 'I . . . I guess so . . . unless something's happened to him,' she replies miserably.

'Maybe the Ogre's got him,' Archie pipes up. This comment earns him a very black look from Kid, who thinks it wise to change the subject.

'Look here, you coots,' he says, 'did any of you happen to get an unsigned card through the letter box yesterday? There was no post so it must have been put through by hand.'

The Squire puts up his hand. 'I did.'

'And me,' squeaks Titch. 'Charlie and I got one each.'

'I had one too,' Busker volunteers. 'Mine had a picture of a guitar on it.'

Indy says hers had children from all over the world dancing around a Christmas tree.

'How about you?' Kid asks Sophie.

She nods. 'Mum found it. Made some naff joke about someone mixing up Valentine's Day with Christmas. What about you?'

'Me too. Dad threw it in the fire. He says sending anonymous letters ought to be against the law.'

'Dumb kind of joke, sending out unsigned cards,' Archie says.

Sophie glares at him. 'It wasn't you, was it?'

They all turn to look at him. The whole thing does have an air of an Archie Williams prank about it.

'Not me,' Archie says quickly. 'I got one too. Ask my folks if you don't believe me.'

'So who was it?' Indy says.

'Some nutter with a very poor sense of humour,' The Squire answers dryly.

'A shy bird at any rate,' Kid puts in.

24

Every day Sophie sets out from home to look for her cat. She calls on all the farms in turn, searching all the buildings and outhouses thoroughly, and peers into every nest, burrow and hollow in the surrounding fields. She even ventures into the woods beyond, though she's been strictly forbidden to go in there alone.

Each morning as she comes out of her gate, people point to her and say: 'There she goes. There goes Sophie Miller to look for her cat.' Everyone feels sorry for the little girl with the sad, unChristmassy face. She waited a long time for that cat. And now it's gone. It's a shame! She is offered so many kittens that Baytree Cottage would be overrun if she had said yes to them all. But she doesn't. Not even the adorable, blue-eyed Siamese one offered by the kind Misses Boone. She thanks them and says that if she didn't already have a cat . . . It's beautiful, enchanting, but it's not her cat, could never be her cat, could never take TC's place in her heart.

Back at the farm once more Sophie slips into the goatshed, hoping against hope that TC has returned and is at this very moment recovering from his adventures, curled up with Benny, Max and Yoghurt. She trains her eyes on the corner of the shed where the barncats have their home. Three pairs of yellow eyes stare back at her. None of them belongs to TC. Her hopes crushed yet again, she is desperate for a shoulder to cry on. She finds two. Kneeling down by Millie and Frieda, she flings her arms around their necks and just cries and cries.

The two goats regard her with clear, amber eyes. Taking a mouthful each of sweater between their spongy lips, they calmly begin to chew at it. Sophie feels them tugging, but leaves them be. They can unravel it all for all she cares. The only thing she wants is for TC to come home, to sleep in the crook of her arm, tunnel in her hair, softly pat her awake in the morning. 'Hurry up and come back, TC,' she implores the missing cat, her tears soaking into Millie's and Frieda's rough flanks.

At tea Sophie doesn't touch the freshly baked scones her mother has placed in front of her. Head bent low over the table, she stares into her plate, lips tight, eyelashes wet with tears.

'Come on, pet, eat something,' her mother pleads. 'Really, there's nothing to be gained by making yourself ill. Your cat will come back, you'll see.'

'I'll never see him again,' Sophie moans, all choked up, her pale face twisted into a mask of despair.

'Now, now, then. No need to take such a desperate view of things,' her father retorts in a matter-of-fact way. 'TC's just having a good time somewhere. Like your mum says, he'll be back.'

'But what if Stone's got him?' she blurts out, and

before she knows it she's telling them about the two visits to his house and the caged animals, snares, traps and cruel-looking instruments lying about the kitchen. Lastly she tells them all about the night she and Kid were going to run away including Farmer Jones's part in it.

When she's finished her parents regard her with grave faces. 'You had no right to do what you did,' her father says frostily. 'Forcing yourselves into a man's home like that! Why, it's nothing short of breaking and entering, a criminal offence, yet you and Kid Brown were going to do it a second time! The whole thing is simply unbelievable. Preposterous!'

Sophie hangs her head. 'It was my idea,' she confesses.

'Fancy leaving a defenceless old man like that in the middle of nowhere to face God knows what,' her father continues, seething with indignation.

'And what if The Beast had gone for you?' her mother puts in.

Sophie wonders why grown-ups always go on so about what didn't happen. 'Well, he didn't,' she mumbles, 'and we did see the animals and all those awful instruments and things and . . .'

'That will do,' her father interrupts stiffly, and Sophie, seeing the storm gathering in his eyes, stops right there.

'Now,' he goes on more kindly. 'I think you and your friends have simply allowed your imaginations to work overtime as regards Farmer Stone. What you saw in his kitchen might well have a logical explanation.'

Sophie, tightening her lips, does not reply. She knows what she has seen.

'What do you think we should do?' Mrs Miller asks her husband.

'Don't know we should do anything.'

'Not even find out for ourselves if Jones is there?'

Mr Miller looks uncertain. 'Let's give it a little longer. Could be his daughter did come and take him to her for the holidays. We don't want to risk making a nuisance of ourselves over nothing, do we?'

'Couldn't we stroll over to Yew Tree Farm on some pretext or other?'

'Like what?'

'Wish him a happy New Year, invite him for a drink, anything.'

'We could do that without it seeming too odd, but I can't say I relish the idea.'

Her mother looks thoughtful. 'Look,' she says, 'a few more days and it will be New Year's Eve. If the old boy is all right, he's sure to be back by then, wherever he is.'

'How's that?'

'He always sees the New Year in at The White Cat, doesn't he?'

Mr Miller looks impressed. 'Well done, Watson.'

Mrs Miller gives him a superior look. 'Holmes, actually.'

'OK, Holmes, then,' her husband concedes. Then adds, 'So, we wait?'

'I think so,' 'Holmes' says, drawing deeply on a non-existent pipe.

Sophie thinks them silly. Also she can't understand

why they should wait. You don't wait when every second counts, when every minute, day, hour that passes could mean the difference between life and death for the hapless animals (including her own cat, which, she is convinced, has been caught by the Ogre, locked up, starved, perhaps even already been experimented on), not to mention Old Jones, who for all they know might already have been served up to The Beast. In spite of what Kid says, to a dog a bone is a bone . . . is a bone!

There is no doubt in Sophie's mind that Stone is guilty of everything he is accused of: shooting Jack, trapping, imprisoning and torturing all kinds of creatures, and of kidnapping. Why else has there been no sign of life from Old Jones for a whole ten days? She for one doesn't believe he's in London. Stone's got him, all right. Hard to believe that someone so bad is living in their midst! But any day now things **will** come to a head. The village **will** march on the criminal, Constable Brown **will** arrest him, he **will** be put behind bars and for all she cares, he can stay there till he rots!

25

New Year's Eve dawns crisp and clear. But though it brings more snow, it does not bring Jones. Kid, true to his word, goes to tell his father. On the way to the kitchen, where his parents are busy packing eggs, he stops off in the hall, where the phone is, to ring Sophie and tell her what he's about to do. Then if she wants to she can tell her parents without feeling she's getting him into deep water. He dials her number and waits. Luckily she answers. 'Hi. You alone?' Kid asks, keeping his voice low.

'Yeah. What's up?'

'Remember what I said about I'd tell my dad if Jones hadn't turned up by now?'

'Have you?'

'No, not yet, but I'm about to.'

A long pause follows. For a moment Kid thinks they've been cut off. 'Hello,' he calls into the mouthpiece, 'Hello!'

A small voice, faint and scared-sounding, begins: 'Kid, promise you won't get mad . . .'

Kid doesn't need to hear any more. 'You've already told yours, right?'

'Sorry, Kid. I didn't mean to. It . . . it just came out.'

'Have they spread it about yet?'

'No, I don't think so. They thought they'd wait till New Year's Eve. That's today. Mum's sure he'll be at The White Cat tonight. She says he never misses seeing the New Year in there with the others. She says if he's all right, he'll be there.'

'Don't think I'll wait till then. Might as well get it over with, seeing as I've already made my mind up.'

'You aren't mad at me, then?'

'No. I just wish we'd come clean earlier.'

'Me too. Well, cheers then . . . and good luck.'

'Thanks.'

Kid puts down the receiver. Taking a deep breath, he strides into the kitchen and dives in at the deep end. He talks and talks and talks. Thinking he might as well be hanged for a sheep as a lamb, he holds nothing back. He even puts in the bit about running away – or at least intending to. When he finally stops, the ticking of the kitchen clock, as good as silent normally, sounds as loud as Big Ben. Kid waits for the verbal lashing from his father. What's it to be? Cleaning the chicken run with a touthbrush? Sit out the rest of the school holidays under house arrest, scraping veg? Sentenced to deliver eggs for the next couple of light years? The minutes tick away. The silence in the room is deep, the tension unbearable. For once Kid finds himself actually anticipating with pleasure the sound of his father's voice, explosive with anger, the colour rising in his face, his eyes shooting sparks, the big hands gathering into tight fists. Anything but this silence!

'Dad,' he begins, 'Dad . . .'

His father looks down at him, his face a picture of utter confusion. 'Run away?' he mumbles, and it sounds like a question rather than a statement. 'Run away?' It's as if he's been told something in a foreign language, or given a coded message impossible to break.

'I'm sorry, Dad. I didn't really want to only . . .'

His father holds up his hand. 'It's all right, lad. It's all right. Now you best help your mum get the eggs packed, while I see to other things.' And with that he turns on his heels. Minutes later he has the telephone wires quivering with the news of Old Jones's disappearance. In a daze Kid fills egg box after egg box in silence. He can't believe it, can't figure out what's come over his father. Unless! Could it be? New Year, new beginnings. No. Not a chance. That kind of soft stuff happens only in stories. And yet. Maybe it's a miracle. There's already been one in Upper Catsfield, Soph getting her cat. If one, then why not two? Or three even? All good things are supposed to come in threes, aren't they? How about Jones turning up safe and sound, or Farmer Stone suddenly sprouting a pair of wings, or both. Now, that would be *some* New Year!

26

By the afternoon the village green is swarming with people. Excitement is running high. A posse has been put together and is waiting for the order to march from Constable Brown. The men want to take their guns along but Constable Brown is quick to stamp out any idea like that. 'We wouldn't want for anyone to get hurt, would we?' he says jovially, rocking back and forth on the heels of his highly polished regulation boots, hands clasped together behind his back.

'Come on, Constable. It'll only be for show. Put the wind up him, like.'

'Show the rogue we mean business.'

'Get him wise to who's who around here.'

'Play tough, I say. Play tough.'

None of this cuts any ice with the constable. 'That's as maybe,' he says, 'only in my experience guns have a habit of going off when held by eager hands. Afterwards no one ever knows how it happened.'

'What about Stone, then? He's bound to have his gun on him,' someone calls out.

'We'll deal with that when and if it occurs,' Kid's

dad says in his stolid, unruffled policeman's voice. 'And now, gentlemen, let's get this show on the road, if you please.'

'Just a moment,' Sophie's mother shouts. 'Shouldn't I call the RSPCA before we go. There might be animals there needing attention.' Everyone agrees, as long as she's quick about it – it's cold outside. They begin to stamp their feet to stop them turning into blocks of ice. Blow Stone . . . And Old Jones too!

Back in the house Sophie's mother gets through to the RSPCA offices in I'chester. She informs them quickly of what's been going on and what they are about to do.

'But,' the voice at the other end begins.

Mrs Miller, normally such a sensible woman, is not to be interrupted. 'Constable Brown is coming along too, so it's all legal,' she says crisply.

'But, but.'

'Thank you. We'll be careful.'

'But, madam, Farmer Stones's . . .'

Again she cuts him off. 'Dangerous. Very dangerous. Especially now he's got poor Mr Jones.'

'But . . .'

'Sorry I've got to rush. Now you will come, won't you? God knows what state those poor animals are in. It's possible some of them might have to be put down.'

At last the posse sets across the white fields in the direction of Yew Tree Farm, armed with pitchforks and cricket bats in place of guns – a bunch of big men with grim faces framed by woolly balaclavas, collars turned up against the cold, hands wrapped tightly round their 'weapons'; upright citizens in a mean mood, determined to see justice done.

Behind them is a long line of hangers-on, respectable folk come along for a spot of sport, and trailing some way behind them are the eight young instigators of the whole affair. Their minds, however (at least for now) are not on Farmer Stone but on what punishment each one has received for his or her part in it. Kid, still not believing (or understanding) his luck, tells them he thought he was sure he'd have to deliver eggs till doomsday. 'I mean, Dad's come down harder on me for less,' he ends in a voice still edged with wonder.

'Perhaps you standing up to him like that has made him think of you differently,' Sophie suggests.

Kid says nothing but he does cross his fingers behind hs back. 'How about you?' he asks her.

'I'll be general dogsbody round the farm for a while. It's a bore but it could have been worse, so I'm not complaining.'

'I am,' Archie moans. 'I'll have to walk to school till Easter.'

'Us too,' call out The Squire, Titch, Sprat, Busker and Indy. They stare at each other in amazement.

'I smell conspiracy,' The Squire mutters darkly.

'Sneaky lot, parents,' Busker agrees.

'Don't know what you're making such a song and dance about,' Kid says to them. 'Walking's no hardship. It's fun.'

Sophie is quick to back him up. 'Yup. Bags of fun.'

'Might be for you two. You're used to it,' Titch sulks

'Walking's boring,' Sprat protests.

'I'll be missing all that TV,' Archie says mournfully.

'I agree with Sprat,' Busker says. 'Walking *is* boring.'

'Stop whimpering like a bunch of infants,' Kid lashes out. 'You'll have us to walk with, won't you? It won't be half as bad as you think. There's lots of fun to be had along that lane.'

'Like what?' Archie sneers.

Kid winks at Sophie. 'Like jumping puddles, for instance.'

'Jumping puddles? What's that?'

'You'll see,' Sophie says, looking all mysterious, her voice packed with promise.

There they stop chatting and, realizing they've fallen a good bit behind the rest, they run to catch them up.

27

After a long tramp over many fields the posse, backed by the body of hangers-on, stands before the gates of Yew Tree Farm. They look about them, sniffing the air like a pack of bloodhounds. Above them the clouds are heavy with snow. A muffled silence lies over the land. It's as if everything is holding its breath. Slowly, step by careful step, they close in on the villain's lair. Constable Brown is raising his arm to knock on the door when it is thrown open, and there in the doorway, filling it, is the man himself, Farmer Stone, gun levelled straight into the centre of the crowd. For a minute no one moves. Then the Constable, assessing the situation, coughs, shuffles his feet and says, ever so politely but with plenty of authority, 'Now then, sir. Perhaps you will be so kind as to lower that there gun.'

Stone gives the constable a long hard look, then, to the amazement of everyone, he actually *gives* his gun to Constable Brown! And now that the big man is no longer a threat, the crowd surge forward and form a tight ring around Farmer Stone. Glaring menacingly, they begin to fire questions at him.

'Where is Old Jones?'

'Where is his dog?'

Stone looks astonished. 'Jones? His dog? Why . . .'

'Don't play the fool with us, mister. We know they're here.'

As if to drive the point home, someone prods Stone in the stomach with the end of a cricket bat.

'Tell us, tell us,' they chant.

'Tell you what?' Stone yells.

'Don't you sound off with us,' the crowd warns him.

Mr Williams, Archie's dad, takes it upon himself to make clear their demands. 'The truth, you blackguard,' he yells. 'The truth.'

The others quickly take up the chant: 'The truth, the truth.'

'What truth?' Stone booms.

'Maybe you shot Old Jones, like you did his dog,' a woman calls grimly. Another roar, like an avalanche gathering speed, rises from the crowd.

'We want Jones,' someone else shouts, and the call is instantly taken up. 'We want Jones, we want Jones.'

'Where is he?'

'Where's his dog?'

'Where's my dog?'

'My cat?'

'My canary?'

'My white mouse?'

'My hamster?'

'Villain! We know you torture animals.'

'Experiment on them.'

'Skin them alive.'

'Feed them to your dog.'

'. . . Keep them locked up.'

'You are all crazy,' Stone bellows.

Sophie, Kid, Sprat, Buster, Titch, The Squire, Archie and Indy are picked out and propelled to the front of the crowd, right in front of Stone.

'No use denying it. These children here saw you with their own eyes.'

'Listen to me,' Stone shouts again. But no one is in the mood to listen to anyone except themselves. Someone pushes a fist under his nose.

'Own up, mister!'

'I have got nothing to say,' Stone cries defiantly.

'Oh yes, you do.'

'No, I don't.'

'Yes, you do.'

The children giggle. It's just like a Christmas panto.

28

Just when it seems that things are getting nowhere, a dog comes hurtling out of the shadows, snarling and growling, jaws gaping, wide lips curled back over a set of fearsome teeth. The crowd leaps back, ready to cut and run. Somebody shouts, 'For God's sake, shoot!' Stone tries to go to the aid of his dog, but he is held back by too many hands. Constable Brown raises the gun, takes aim and . . . Just as he pulls the trigger a van – the letters RSPCA emblazoned on the side – screeches to a halt between the gun and the dog. The bullet meant for Stone's beast bores into the vehicle's side. A man, his face white with shock, jumps out and without further ado knocks the gun out of the constable's hands.

'You raving lunatic. What the blazes do you think you're playing at? You could have killed me,' he shouts, shaking with rage and not caring at all that he is addressing a policeman.

Constable Brown draws himself up to his full height and says stiffly, 'As the representative of law and order in this here village, I have every right to act in the interests of public safety by putting down this here dangerous animal.'

'It's you and those fools with you who should be put down,' the newcomer thunders. He dives behind the van, reappearing immediately with The Beast, his hand around the dog's collar. With a sharp intake of breath the crowd draws back. Taking not the slightest notice of them, The Beast tears himself free and jumps up at Stone, licking him and uttering short, anxious yelps.

'So, so, boy,' Stone says softly. He looks at the hostile faces before him. 'It's all right. He won't harm anyone,' he assures them.

People stare at one another. Why, the man sounds almost human!

Sophie thinks now is the time to ask Farmer Stone the question uppermost in *her* mind. 'Farmer Stone, what have you done with my cat?'

'Your cat, girl?'

'Yes.'

'Your cat?' Stone repeats.

'Yes,' she answers impatiently, 'my cat. A black tom with the greenest eyes you've ever seen.'

'Aah,' Stone exclaims softly. It's not the reply Sophie has hoped for. 'I, I hope you ha – haven't shot him or . . . or skinned him,' she stammers.

Stone looks genuinely puzzled. 'Shot, skinned?'

'Well, you did shoot his mother. At least, I'm sure it was you,' she bursts out, her eyes bright with tears.

Stone stares at her for a long time, as if trying to recall something that happened long ago. 'A white cat?' he asks at last.

Sophie nods. She doesn't trust herself to speak.

'My hunch was right, then,' he says, speaking

more to himself than to her.

'He is admitting to it,' people whisper to one another. 'He actually admits he shot the Millers' cat.'

People have been quiet since The Beast appeared on the scene but now, suddenly remembering why they are here, they grow restive again. 'Where is Jones? Where is he?' The call 'We want Jones' is revived.

Mr Jackson, the man from the RSPCA, puts himself between Stone and the posse. 'Thank you, Mr Jackson,' Stone says, but I think maybe I owe these people an explanation.

'Not before time,' is the general response.

'Listen, all of you,' Stone calls out. 'It's true I shot the white cat this little girl's talking about.'

The crowd drowns his words with a new roar. Stone puts up his hand.

'It's also true I've trapped all kinds of animals in my time and, yes, skinned them too – though not alive,' he adds hastily.

An expectant silence settles over the yard. Taking a deep breath Stone continues. 'But I have never carried out experiments on any animals, nor do I kidnap people. I've been bad, very bad, but that's all in the past.' He looks at Mr Jackson, who nods as if *he* knows what it's all about. 'I'll start at the beginning,' he says shyly.

'Best place,' someone pipes up.

'Every man who is angry feels himself hurt,' Stone begins. 'In fact, just remembering how hurt I was helped to make me angrier still. It all began when I was a boy. I'd always longed for a pet, a dog or a cat, but as we had only a small flat, and lived in a big town at that, my parents said no. Well, I had quite given up the idea of ever having a pet of my own when my aunt made me a present of a pup. She told my mother I was much too lonely and that having an animal to care for would "bring me out of myself". My mother answered that she wasn't going to keep an animal in a flat and that was that, and would my aunt kindly take the dog and leave. Next time they thought of giving me anything they should consult with her first. My aunt left, but without taking the pup. She said if my mum didn't want it, then *she* would have to get rid of it. And that is what happened. When I came back from school that day the puppy was gone. At first my mum said it had run away of its own accord, but I said how could it with the door locked? She gave in then and said it had been given to someone in 'the country' and how much happier it would be there than shut up in a flat. I cried and begged her to tell me where they'd taken it, but they said it was better if I didn't know. It would make it easier for me to forget.'

Stone looks above and beyond the heads of the crowd, his eyes dark with the old pain. Suddenly everyone feels sorry for him. They can see this opening of an old wound is painful for him.

After a short pause Stone takes up the story again. 'Anyway, up till then I had been what is called a "good" child. The business with the dog changed all that. I was convinced that in not wanting the pup my parents didn't want me either. How else could they have hurt me so? Sadly, it didn't stop with them.

Suddenly I felt everyone, the whole world, was against me. In the beginning I often felt ashamed of the meanness I showed to the children who had been my friends. Especially those I knew had pets at home. If I walked past them in the street or happened to come across them with their dogs or cats, I pretended not to see them. But if I stopped "seeing" them, they also stopped "seeing" me. Soon I no longer had anyone I could call my friend. I told myself that I didn't care, that I didn't want anyone to like me – it made it easier for me to not like them.

'It got so bad my parents decided a change of scene might do me good. The place they picked was a farm. They reasoned that being with animals all the time would make up for me not having any of my own. But, as sometimes happens, even the most well-intentioned schemes go terribly wrong. And so it was with me. I loathed the animals from the very first day. Just being near a dog or a cat was enough to make me feel ill. I told the farmer I wanted nothing to do with them. So to occupy me he taught me how to shoot and when I was good enough, he let me loose on the so-called "vermin" he said was ruining his crops and eating him out of house and home. I didn't need to be asked twice. That summer I killed so much "vermin" I got to have nightmares about it: rabbits, stoats, badgers, squirrels, foxes, crows, rooks, sparrows, robins. My hard heart knew no bounds. I had not been born a wolf, but I allowed myself to become one. I grew up morose, sullen, antisocial, friendless – a hater of other human beings.'

Stone is boring his eyes into the crowd. 'Hatred is

so lasting and so stubborn,' he tells them, underlining every word, 'that it needs a miracle to shift it.' His eyes move to The Beast. Luckily a miracle came my way, and of all things it was in the shape of a small dog. To cut a long story short, I'd just dumped some unwanted stuff at the local tip when, from the top of it a black plastic bag, the kind used for rubbish, came rolling down to land at my feet. But instead of just lying there, it began to move. Curious to see what was making a perfectly ordinary plastic bag behave in such an odd manner I bent down and untied the rope holding it shut. No sooner had I done this than a dog, no more than a pup, shot out and set to licking my hands.' Stone points to The Beast. 'Poor cur. Not hard to imagine what was in store for him had I not happened to come along when I did. Anyway, I'd done my bit, or so I told myself; I'd rescued him from his bag and the rest of his life was no concern of mine. I began to walk back to my car. It simply did not occur to me to take him with me. Well, I'd not taken more than a couple of steps when he started whimpering and whining fit to soften the hardest heart. At any rate he managed to melt the ice in mine and, well, we've been together ever since. To begin with we lived in the town, but when I realized just how big he was going to be, I decided town was no place for a dog like him.'

Stone looks sheepishly at the upturned faces before him. 'Remember the beginning of this tale?'

Archie, however, is not that easily brought round. 'So you came to Upper Catsfield to carry on hunting animals and . . . and frightening kids,' he says, accusingly.

'I know that's how it looks, but in fact, thanks to The Beast, I'd decided to turn over a new leaf before I came here,' Stone answers, not in the least offended.

Sprat looks sceptical. 'Didn't seem like it that day we crashed into you in the lane.'

Stone scratches his head. 'Well, er, you did come on me rather suddenly if I may say so. I tried to speak to you but the whole lot of you looked like you'd turned to stone.'

'No wonder. You looked a right og– I mean, you were real scary,' Indy dares.

Stone grins, 'What you don't know is that I was as frightened of you as you were of me.'

'You can't be serious,' they respond with one voice, amazed at their own daring. 'I am too,' he assures them. They stare at him, not sure what to make of it. The Ogre scared of them. Some horror story it's turning out to be.

'If you really had turned over a new leaf, then how come you shot our cat?' Sophie says curtly.

A look of genuine repentance crosses Stone's face. 'I didn't mean to kill the white cat,' he says sadly. 'It was an accident. She was a beautiful animal. Fact is, I adore white cats. When I found one had chosen to make her home in my barn, I did all I could to make her welcome. I told The Beast he was to leave her alone, put down sacks and straw for her for a nest and brought her fresh milk to drink. I'll never know why – perhaps I moved too quickly and frightened her – but she went for me, digging her claws into the back of my hand and leaving a deep, bloody gash right across it. I think it was the sudden pain made me act as I did. I grabbed my gun and let off a shot. I wasn't aiming to hit her. I only meant to vent some of my anger on her. What happened, though, was she shot out of the barn – to draw me away from her young, I guess – and across the fields, with me after her, just as I was, coatless, hatless, braces hanging.

Sophie points to herself and Kid. 'We saw you, only we thought you were after a rabbit.'

Stone nods miserably.

'When did you know you had hit her?'

'Not till much later, I'm afraid.' I was sitting in the barn waiting for her to return, all ready to put things right with a saucer of cream, when there's a noise from the direction of her nest. I crept over to it and there she was, standing over her young, her lovely white coat streaked with blood. The moment she saw me she grabbed one of them in her mouth and was off before I could get to her. I rushed after her, certain she wouldn't get far, what with being hurt and with a kitten to slow her down. But somehow she managed to give me the slip. I must have tramped through every field between here and I'chester looking for them, but it was no use. I found not the slightest trace of the white cat and her child. It was as if the ground had opened up and swallowed them. I returned home empty-handed. I spent the night hidden in the barn, hoping against hope she might come back. In the morning, when there was still no sign of her, I brought the rest of the litter into the house. The Beast helped me to raise them.'

He stoops down to pat The Beast. 'Believe me,' he announces proudly 'those kittens could not have wished for a better foster-mother. And, as they say, there's no loss without some kind of gain. In my case, deeply as I regretted the whole business, it did set me thinking about what happens to abandoned or orphaned creatures. I'd already given the question some thought after finding The Beast and now I acted on it. I called the RSPCA in I'chester, told them about myself and asked if they might have some use for me. The outcome was that Mr Jackson here said he was prepared to give me a chance.

'Best thing I ever did,' the RSPCA man confirms.

'So,' Stone continues, 'though it is true to say I still hunt, nowadays it is to save animals not destroy them.' Without further ado he steps up to Sophie and takes her hand. 'I think I have something of yours you'd very much like to have back,' he tells her.

Off they go. Stone and Sophie in front, followed by Kid, Sprat, Titch, Busker, The Squire, Indy and Archie Williams, with the adults at the rear. Without as much as a whisper of explanation, Stone marches them into the cottage and straight to the kitchen. To the children it looks just as it did on the night of 'Operation Special Delivery'. The traps, snares, hypodermics, scalpels and bottles with poison labels are all there. Cages, most of them occupied by small animals or birds, hang from hooks in the ceiling like weird chandeliers. Even the three cats they glimpsed that fateful night are huddled together on the same chair as then.

'Snowflake's children,' Titch mouths to the others.

'He's telling the truth,' The Squire whispers to Archie out of the corner of his mouth.

'Don't be so sure,' Archie sneers. He isn't going to let his guard down, not just yet anyway, even if everyone else is.

'Then how is it you still keep animals locked up if you like them so much now?' he demands insolently.

A smile flits across Farmer Stone's face. 'Still doubting, eh?' He smiles in a good-humoured way. 'But to answer your question, it is for their own good. You see, the animals in these cages are all in various stages of recovery.'

Suddenly he is at the door. 'If you'll excuse me for just a moment,' he says, pushing past the throng of people blocking the doorway. They hear him climbing the stairs, first up – from the sound of it seems he's taking them two at a time – then down, more cautiously, as if he is carrying something precious. He is back only minutes later, holding what looks like a cat basket high over his head. He sets it down on the table. 'Talking of recovery,' he pants somewhat out of breath, 'I have a patient here who will be glad to see someone very special to him.'

'TC!' Sophie throws herself over the basket. Never has there been a happier little girl. Through the bars on the door of the cage a black cat, looking as if it has been dragged backwards through a shredder is regarding her with cool, emerald-green eyes.

A murmur goes through the crowd. 'It is . . . yes . . . no doubt about it. It is Tooth and Claw, Snowflake's child, Sophie Miller's cat.'

'I put him in there to keep him away from the other cats. I'm afraid they don't take kindly to intruders and it just wouldn't do for him to get into a fight the way he is,' Stone explains.

Sophie glances at Kid. She is telling him that she knew he would have come home if he had been able to. She turns back to Stone. 'Where did you find him?'

'Crying outside my front door. I opened it and there he was.' Farmer Stone shakes his head at the memory. 'I looked him over and decided I would not be able to do anything for him, he was so badly torn. I got a syringe ready, telling myself there was nothing for it but to put him to sleep, but at the crucial moment, he turned those incredible eyes of his on me and well . . . I don't mind admitting, I just couldn't go through with it. I put down the syringe and peered more closely at him. It was then I remembered another cat, a white cat with the same piercing green eyes – and the night she took off with a tiny black kitten dangling from her mouth. And I think, can it be? Is this that same black kitten? Am I being given a chance to make up for the terrible wrong I did him and his mother that awful day? Am I to get peace of mind on that score at least?' He looks first at Sophie then at the other children. 'It's enough to make you believe in miracles, don't you think?'

Sophie, her eyes taking stock of TC's injuries, nods. A miracle for sure. You only have to look at her cat. A plastic collar has been put round his neck to stop him from getting to the nasty wound on his back, one ear is badly torn, there's an ugly gash across his nose and both front legs are heavily bandaged. She asks Farmer Stone how come TC's in such a sorry state.

'Going by the nature of the wounds I'd say he must have had a run-in with a fox,' Stone replies, then adds, 'By the way, I had to dig out quite a few lead pellets from his rear end too, though I don't know who it was put those in him.'

Sophie bites her lip. She's certain she does. Still, all's well that ends well. Hopefully that experience has put TC off any future raids on strange kitchens. In fact she's certain of it. She doesn't think TC will put himself up as a target for Uncle Morris ever again.

Aloud she asks, 'May I take him home?'

'No reason why not, only keep the collar on him a while longer. Wouldn't be good for him to get to the wound on his back for a while yet.'

Sophie takes TC out of the basket and hugs him to her. 'I will, and thank you for taking care of him, Farmer Stone.'

'Thank you,' he returns and, looking at the black cat, 'and thank you too, young fellow. It means a lot to me that you didn't perish along with your poor mother – and to have been the one to nurse you back to health, even if right now you do look somewhat worse for wear.'

Stone's uninvited guests no longer know whether they are standing on their heads or their heels. What a day of surprises it's turned out to be. And there's more to come. Gesturing to them to follow him, he battles his way through the mass of people that have collected in the hallway outside the kitchen and goes through to the lounge. Not the dark, grimy, cheerless hole that everyone has imagined but a bright room hung with streamers, balloons and little lanterns,

with artificial snow on the windows – even though there's plenty of the real stuff outside – and, the biggest surprise of all so far, a Christmas tree decorated with tinsel, yards and yards of it, coloured lights, baubles, odds and ends dangling from golden loops and, on the very top, a beautiful fairy complete with silver crown, magic wand and a dress so fine it might be made out of gossamer.

Stone, clearly pleased with the effect the whole thing is having on his visitors, chuckles softly and, in the voice of someone with a trick or two still up his sleeve announces, 'can't say I'm much for this kind of thing myself, but Jones here as good as insisted on it.'

At the mention of Jones everyone comes to life again. 'Jones?' they exclaim, 'Jones!'

'You did say you wanted to see him, didn't you,' Stone teases. 'Well, then! Here he is.' And with that he strides up to an armchair, grabs hold of the back and, in one movement, turns it round. Fast asleep on it, his cheeks red from the blazing fire in the grate is Old Jones, a large red setter as ancient-looking as himself dozing at his feet. Bending over him, Stone gently shakes the old man awake.

Jones opens his watery eyes and looks about him. Dozens of necks extend towards him for a better view. It's Old Jones all right, without as much as a scratch or a bruise on him. The old man grins at them and sits up. 'My, such grave faces, anyone died?' he cackles.

Archie points to Stone. 'We, we thought he might have murdered you and . . . and fed you to The Beast,' he stutters, desperately holding on to his own picture of Stone.

'Or at least kidnapped you,' his father adds loyally.

'Kidnapped, murdered. Goodness me, what nonsense. You people have some funny notions and no mistake,' the old man says, astonished. 'Why, Stone here couldn't have looked after me better or made more fuss of me if I had been his own grandpappy.' At that very moment his eyes fall on Sophie and Kid. 'You there, heartless whipper-snappers,' he croaks, shaking a bony finger at them. 'If you really believed Stone to be a kidnapper, murderer and goodness knows what else besides, how do you explain running off and leaving an old man to face such a monster singlehanded, eh? Eh?'

The two children turn crimson. 'So-Sorry,' they stammer. 'We really are sorry we ran out on you.'

'Well, I'm not,' Farmer Jones says cheerfully, 'I've had a spiffing time. Best Christmas ever!'

Busker points to Jack. 'Where was he, then? He's been gone so long we all thought he'd snuffed . . . I mean, we thought he was dead.'

Mr Jackson steps forward. 'I can explain.' He goes on to tell them Jack had been knocked down by a car half way to I'chester (a mystery how he came to be so far from home) and was taken to the RSPCA there. They'd thought of putting him to sleep but hadn't, though by rights they could have, seeing he was not wearing a collar. Instead they'd operated on him and put him in plaster and then waited for someone to come along and claim him. But no one did. There had been a couple of calls about lost setters, but when people called in to look at him he was always the wrong one. Because of his age they knew it would be almost impossible to find a home for him and again discussed putting him down. As luck would have it, Stone called at the eleventh hour, offering his services. It was decided to give him the setter as a kind of test. If he could put an animal as hurt as this one back on its feet, he was the man for them. Stone did not seem daunted by the task. He picked up the dog and took him to Upper Catsfield, little knowing he was taking him home, so to speak.

Mr Jackson gives Jack a thoughtful look. 'It's possible he might have tried to make it back to his master had he not been in plaster. Anyway, in the end his master came to him. A miracle I call it, yes, a miracle.'

29

The eight steal veiled glances at one another. So it had been Jack and not The Beast they'd heard barking on the night of 'Operation Special Delivery'. He must have been in one of the bedrooms upstairs. No wonder Sprat had thought the sound had come from somewhere within the cottage! To think they'd been thrown into a blue funk by a dog hardly able to move even its tail. How humiliating! What unnecessary trouble they'd brought on themselves: breaking into Yew Tree Farm, Kid and Sophie almost running away, their well-meaning but ill-conceived and ill-timed second visit to Stone's to help animals which, as it turns out, had no need of their help. Then there was Sophie's agony at the disappearance of her cat, and for all of them, a Christmas spent on tenter-hooks. They'll be careful to check their facts before rushing into any more adventures!

Anyway, it's all over now and many things are better for it. The chain of nightmares has been broken. There'll be no more sleepless nights now, no tossing and turning in their beds, no gory visions of mangled little bodies, human or animal.

Still, it's kind of hairy to think how ugly things

might have turned out, especially if Mr Jackson had not come when he did and stopped Constable Brown shooting The Beast. It's anyone's guess what would have happened then. Sophie, feeling she is to blame for things getting out of hand, thinks this is the time to apologize to Farmer Stone.

'Farmer Stone,' she ventures, speaking for them all. 'We've been such clods, real Wurzels. I . . . I guess we allowed our imaginations to get the better of us.'

'Partly my own fault, child,' Stone replies kindly, 'I should have made an effort to get to know you folks when I first came, but being on my own so long has made me shy of people, and it might have stayed like that had Jones not forced himself into my life.'

He stops and laughs long and loud at the memory. 'You should have seen him. After almost breaking my windows and then my door, in he barges like a mad bull, bellowing abuse at the top of his voice, demanding to see Jack or else! Well, I took him upstairs to the room where I kept Jack and asked him if this was the dog he was going on about. You should have seen his face. Dropped right down to his toes. When he recovered, he was like a child with a dream come true. Afterwards, one thing led to another and I ended up inviting him to spend Christmas with me. I tell you, I didn't have to ask twice. Quick as a flash he asks to borrow the phone and calls his daughter in London, telling her not to bother to come for him this year as he'll be spending Christmas with a friend, and has been here since.'

Sophie points to Kid. 'Kid said something like that

but neither of us took it seriously.' She taps the side of her head. 'Loopy, that's what we are.'

'I suggest we call it quits and leave it at that,' Stone suggests.

This generous offer to square things once and for all is gratefully accepted by all, children as well as adults. Everyone is content to put the whole sorry affair behind them.

'By the way,' Stone says shyly, 'I trust you children all got your Christmas cards?'

'So it was you,' they cry in unison. 'But why didn't you sign them?'

Stone takes an envelope from the mantelpiece and waves it at them. 'I might ask the same of you?'

Another shout goes up. 'The letter!'

Stone puts it back. 'That's right. Some eye-opener, if I may say so. That and something that happened to reach my ears when I was walking up the lane once.' And, while everyone is trying to figure out what it can be, Stone, mouth stretched into a broad grin, sings out:

Big bad Stone,
Teeth like tombstones,
Eyes like millstones,
Nose like a squashed toad,
Mouth like a black hole
Gives kids nightmares,
Makes them groan,
Toss and turn –
The Devil take Old Stone!

Eight scarlet faces stare up at him in horror. But Stone

is laughing so much the walls shake: 'Mouth like a black hole . . . nose a squashed toad . . . Fancy that. Ha, ha, ha!'

Plenty of egg on their faces now as they wait for the laughter to subside. Eventually it does. Stone, wiping his eyes, booms, 'I haven't laughed so much since I was a lad. Thank you, thank you all.'

And, having got that out of his system, he moves on to something more serious. 'Now we know one another better, perhaps you will find time to come and give me a hand with the animals now and again. What do you say?'

They are all of them keen, except Archie, who is worrying about the TV he might miss.

'Come on, Archie. Say yes. Give the box a rest.'

Archie still hesitates. He looks up to see Farmer Stone staring at him. The ex-Ogre winks at him.

'Speaking for myself', he says, 'it is amazing what new interests can do for one.'

Archie grins. Something tells him the big man is laughing at himself. Archie likes that. Means the ogre . . . whoops, Farmer Stone is not above cracking a joke. Who knows, maybe they'll get to crack the odd one together even. He holds out his hand. 'OK, I'll have a shot at it,' he promises.

Farmer Stone takes the small, rough hand into his own big and much rougher one. 'Good on you, son. Looking forward to seeing you here.'

'Thank you,' Archie replies, impressed to be shaking hands with an Ogre, even if, like this one, he's been demoted to a mere human.

'And now, how about us all going to The White Cat

to see the New Year in. First round on the house,' Mr King, the publican, calls out.

This meets with approval all round, but before they do go, there's one thing Sophie just has to know. She tugs at Stone's sleeve.

'Farmer Stone, what is your first name?'

'My first name?'

'Yes. You must have a first name. Everyone does.'

He clears his throat. The question has clearly embarrassed him, but he sees he'll have to answer. 'Well, hm . . . hm. If you must know, it's Horatio,' he mutters, his voice scarcely above a whisper. He hates his name, always has. All his life he has been just plain 'Stone'.

He wonders what the child wants with it, but doesn't have long to wait. Sophie stares at the ceiling, chews her lip, screws up her face and, as everyone begins to move towards the door, it comes:

Three cheers for Horatio Stone,
Friend of beasties great and small!
Treats their bruises,
Mends their bones,
No more nightmares,
No more groans.
Happy New Year, Horatio Stone!

The waves of cheers that follow almost take the roof off. When they've died down, people begin to file out of the little cottage, no longer an ogre's lair but the home of a good neighbour everyone is glad to know, and who is glad to know them.

Sophie, cradling TC in her arms, looks into his

damaged face. 'I'm not glad you got hurt but since it happened, I'm glad it was Farmer Stone who found you and patched you up. Now I know him, I shan't worry so much if you ever go missing again.' Bending her head, she gives the point of his tattered ear a little peck. A pink tongue shoots out and delicately touches the tip of her nose. 'Payment in kind,' he seems to be saying.

A delicious warmth steals over Sophie. Right now she feels she has got all she wants. Her mother and father, her friend Kid, plenty of other good friends and neighbours – old and new – and last but by no means least a black, black cat with cool green eyes who came to her one storm-tossed night to share with her all the fun, the happiness and the heartaches of his nine lives.